# A Cruise to Murder

DAWN BROOKES

D0094051

# A Cruise
# to
# Murder

*A Rachel Prince Mystery*

## DAWN BROOKES

*OAKWOOD PUBLISHING*

*www.dawnbrookespublishing.com*

Paperback Edition 2018

Kindle Edition 2018

Paperback ISBN: 978-1-9998575-3-0

Cover Design by Janet Dado

*To my mum*

*The kindest woman I ever knew*

# Table of Contents

*Chapter 1* ........................................................................ *1*

*Chapter 2* ...................................................................... *12*

*Chapter 3* ...................................................................... *25*

*Chapter 4* ...................................................................... *30*

*Chapter 5* ...................................................................... *40*

*Chapter 6* ...................................................................... *45*

*Chapter 7* ...................................................................... *51*

*Chapter 8* ...................................................................... *56*

*Chapter 9* ...................................................................... *70*

*Chapter 10* .................................................................... *82*

*Chapter 11* .................................................................... *89*

*Chapter 12* .................................................................. *103*

*Chapter 13* .................................................................. *110*

*Chapter 14* .................................................................. *120*

*Chapter 15* .................................................................. *129*

*Chapter 16* .................................................................. *139*

*Chapter 17* .................................................................. *152*

*Chapter 18* .................................................................. *155*

*Chapter 19* .................................................................. *159*

*Chapter 20* .................................................................. *171*

_Chapter 21_ ..................................................... _178_

_Chapter 22_ ..................................................... _182_

_Chapter 23_ ..................................................... _188_

_Chapter 24_ ..................................................... _194_

_Chapter 25_ ..................................................... _204_

_Chapter 26_ ..................................................... _211_

_Chapter 27_ ..................................................... _221_

_Chapter 28_ ..................................................... _225_

_Chapter 29_ ..................................................... _228_

_Chapter 30_ ..................................................... _235_

_Chapter 31_ ..................................................... _244_

_Chapter 32_ ..................................................... _248_

_Chapter 33_ ..................................................... _252_

_Other Books by Dawn Brookes_ .........................................

_About the Author_..........................................................

_Acknowledgements_ ........................................................

# Chapter 1

"I can't do this anymore, Rachel. I've met someone else." The words pierced through her brain, like knives carving her in two.

Rachel awoke with a start, wondering where she was. The rhythmic chugging sound of a train on railway tracks reminded her immediately. Pushing the dream to the back of her mind, she looked around the busy train. The middle-aged woman with a teenage girl in tow, who had sat opposite Rachel at the start of her journey, had gone. She had been replaced by a younger woman with customary ear phones attached to her head and eyes glued to the mobile phone in her hand. A young man, presumably her boyfriend, was sitting next to her, reading a book and eating a sandwich.

Rachel noticed that the rather large man who had been sitting in the aisle seat next to her had also been replaced. An older man reading a newspaper was now beside her. Realising that she must have been in a very deep sleep, she automatically checked that her handbag was still in place. She had squashed it between herself and the side of the carriage when her eyes had begun to feel like lead and she realised that sleep was inevitable.

Reassured that it was still there, she took a quick look behind her to where the luggage compartment was and noticed her suitcase remained where she had left it. Vivid pink with white polka dots, it was hardly going to go unnoticed, even though it was now surrounded by other people's luggage. She had bought it to stand out and stand out it did.

Looking at her watch, she saw that it was now ten o'clock in the morning. She turned and looked out of the window, the sadness that had been wrenching her heart for weeks re-surfacing. Work had been busy, and she had pulled in extra hours to help dull the pain, but now she had stopped, it came crashing in on her again.

*Blast Robert – get out of my head,* she thought as tears stung the back of her eyes. Thankfully, phone-girl was too busy with her device to notice the tears.

The passengers around her were eating and drinking, so she assumed she must have missed the trolley service. Another hour and a half and the train would be arriving in Southampton. The smell of fresh coffee made her thirsty, and she needed to stretch her legs. Rachel decided to go for a walk and get some sustenance.

With an involuntary sigh that drew a sympathetic look from the man seated next to her, she excused herself and made her way through the train to the buffet car.

The train was now tearing through the countryside and felt like it was floating on air, except for the occasional shaking of the carriages from side to side. It was much busier than it had been at seven-thirty when she had first boarded in Leeds. The walk became an obstacle course as she fought her way past different-sized luggage overflowing into the aisles. She almost lost her balance as she moved through the carriages and felt the sway where they joined together.

*Why did I agree to this holiday?* She was pondering this thought when she finally arrived at the buffet car. Sarah had been so kind and sympathetic when Rachel had called her two months ago after Robert had decided to end their relationship and leave her broken-hearted and alone. Rachel had been engaged to Robert for a year, but she had noticed a change in him about six months prior to the breakup. At the time, distracted by assessments and not really able deal with it, she had put it down to the work strain they were both under and dismissed his moodiness.

Robert worked in Manchester as a police sergeant. They had met at a party and were immediately attracted to each other, discovering that they both went to church and were both in the police force. He had approached her while she was sitting with a group of friends.

"Would you like to dance?" It wasn't the best pickup line she had heard, but from the moment she looked into his dark-green eyes, she was smitten. It had seemed to be an ideal match, and it had been as far as Rachel was concerned.

Rachel had recently joined the force when they first met and was committed to staying in Leeds until her two years as a student officer were completed. Robert had been supportive initially, and when he asked her to marry him, she was over the moon. They agreed that she would look for work in Manchester once she qualified as constable.

*That was before – this is now.* Sorrow and pain coursed through her veins.

She bought herself a rather stale club sandwich and a cup of strong coffee and felt a bit better for having something to eat and drink. Grateful that she was not one of those people who starved themselves when they were unhappy, she was equally aware that she did not want to comfort eat and gain weight – especially being a fitness fanatic. Even she had stopped eating for a few days following the shock announcement from Robert eight weeks earlier though.

The memories once again invaded her senses.

She had gone to visit him in Manchester, and as usual arrived at his sister's house. Robert's sister, Louise, lived around the corner from his flat. She was a kind and patient woman with three children under the age of five and a husband who seemed to work all hours. Louise was committed to family life although Rachel couldn't help noticing that she looked exhausted most of the time.

Rachel sometimes wondered if her husband deliberately missed getting home early in order to avoid having to spend time with the children or help with chores. She'd convinced herself that Robert would not be like that, and they would live as loving partners.

*At least we would have done, if he'd got over his moodiness and more importantly, if he hadn't met someone else.*

Rachel had arrived late on that Friday night and only seen him briefly.

"I'll collect you tomorrow morning at ten. We'll go out for lunch and spend the day together." He turned away before she could kiss him.

Her time was limited as she had to get back to Leeds on Saturday night to work on the Sunday. Looking back, she realised how foolish she had been, missing all the warning signs; but she had been studying frantically to finish her police assessments while planning for the future, and she was madly in love.

Louise had seemed quiet and distant over breakfast on the Saturday morning.

"Is everything alright?" Rachel wondered if she and her husband, George, had argued. George had left early in the morning and, unusually, had given Rachel a hug before he went.

"Yes, fine. I just need to get the children ready for their grandma." Louise had busied herself in the kitchen for the rest of the morning.

Robert arrived at around eleven o'clock, an hour later than they'd agreed. He didn't apologise for being late.

"I've only got time for lunch," he said brusquely.

"Oh, that's a shame. I was hoping we could go into town." She was disappointed, but tried to hide it, naively thinking he must have been called in to work – not unusual for police officers. Although a staunch believer in people's rights to protest, march, and all manner of other things, Rachel did sometimes wish they would spare a thought for the police. The police had to give up their days off and time with families to maintain public order. Even the most peaceful demonstrations could erupt into violence if rival factions got over-heated.

Robert was quiet again.

"I've just got the one assessment left to do next week and then I'll be qualified. It won't be long before we can spend a lot more time together." Rachel tried to make the most of the time they had, overcompensating for his lack of speech by babbling on. They stopped outside her favourite café; the familiar smell of percolated coffee and baking filled her senses with a pleasing aroma. She entered the premises happily, looking forward to a romantic lunch, but Robert seemed to move away whenever she tried to hold his hand.

"I missed every signal. I was blind," she later told Sarah.

There was the usual queue of people waiting to be served, and they waited in line to order lunch and coffees. Rachel ordered her favourite home-made beef and potato pie and was about to tuck in when Robert grabbed her hand.

*At last, some sign of affection.* Then she looked into his eyes with a feeling of foreboding. He stared at her with a coldness she had not seen before; she was looking into someone else's eyes – these were not the happy eyes of her fiancé.

"I can't do this anymore, Rachel. I've met someone else. I love her and I want to marry her."

He threw himself back into the chair and took a deep breath. At this point, he looked away.

Rachel couldn't believe what she was hearing – her stomach was in knots and her heart was racing. Beginning to feel light-headed, she opened her mouth but realised she couldn't speak.

Taking advantage of the fact that she was unable to say anything, Robert continued. "I've tried, Rachel, really I have. I met Jessica through an inter-church thing – we started doing youth clubs together and things developed from there."

Rachel saw a look in his eyes that had once belonged to her as he began to speak about this woman whom he had dared to give a name. Somehow, thinking of this person as the other woman allowed Rachel to feel angry; but thinking of her as Jessica brought her to life as another person who had fallen in love with a man. Rachel's man.

Flabbergasted, Rachel shut down and went into autopilot. She could thank her police training for this skill because it helped her to survive the conversation – and it had become a matter of her survival. Her hand felt sore, and she realised that she had been twisting her engagement ring round and round while he was speaking.

"I need to go to the bathroom," she said, and then she got up and walked straight out of the café. At first, she didn't know where she was going, but after about an hour she realised she was heading for the train station. Her mobile phone had rung a few times with Robert's ringtone, but she declined the calls and turned it off. She knew she was not being very adult about this, but her heart had just been torn apart.

*How else should I react?* she asked herself, angrily. Tears fell down her face as she walked, and she had to use every ounce of strength to stop herself from sobbing in the street. A few people looked at her as she passed by with embarrassed fleeting glances, but no-one had asked if she was alright.

Sorrow had turned to anger by the time she reached the train station – anger with Robert for doing this to her, and anger at herself for missing all the warning signs. She saw that there was a train leaving for Leeds in ten minutes, so she sprinted to the platform.

Once on the train, Rachel had found a quiet compartment, unusual for a Saturday. She sat down and tried to take in all that had happened over the few hours that had been spent with Robert. Her happy, stable life had been thrown into turmoil, and she felt terrified of the fragility that overwhelmed her. The dark and devastating thoughts scrambling through her brain were totally new.

*If only I had recognised the signs over the previous six months for what they were, the pain might have been a bit less and I might have been better prepared for what just occurred.* She felt betrayed, angry, dreadfully sad; but most of all, she felt stupid. Her father had tried to warn her about long-distance relationships – not that Leeds and Manchester were that far apart.

"I am sure it will all work out for you," he had said after her engagement. "But just be aware that people can change, and you haven't known him that long."

Robert had asked her father's permission before proposing in the traditional way, and he had given it without hesitation. Rachel's dad, Brendan Prince, was a vicar in Hertfordshire where Rachel had been brought up. Robert had joked with her later, saying that her father had warned him: "Don't you hurt my daughter or you will have me to answer to." They had laughed about it then, but now Rachel wondered whether her wonderful dad had seen something in Robert that she couldn't or wouldn't see.

*I don't suppose he asked my dad for permission to break off the engagement,* she thought bitterly. *How do I tell my parents?*

When she got back to her flat, she realised she hadn't let Louise know that she wasn't going to collect her overnight bag. She turned her phone on and saw fourteen missed calls and numerous texts from Robert, all of which she deleted.

There was a text from Louise which read: *"I am so sorry, Rachel, for what has happened. We only knew about it yesterday as Robert had kept it all to himself. Please let me know you are okay, I understand you will be angry and upset. The children send hugs and kisses."*

Rachel replied: *"Thanks, Louise, I have returned to Leeds. Sorry to leave without saying goodbye, but had to get away and take it all in. Love to the boys."*

She received a sympathetic reply, but they had not communicated since, except when Louise had sent a parcel with her overnight bag and a *thinking of you* card. Robert had tried to call a few more times, but she had not replied. He did write one letter, which still lay unopened in her suitcase. She might open it with Sarah.

*If only I hadn't joined the police force, I would never have met Robert.* She knew it was silly to think that way, but her head was still reeling from the shock.

"You alright, love?" A voice behind her brought her back to the present. She had been staring out of the window opposite the buffet bar and hadn't realised there were tears streaming down her face. She gathered herself together, looking up at the buffet car attendant.

"Yes, I'm fine, thank you," she replied. *Pull yourself together*, she chastised herself, and then she made her way back through the train to her seat, after washing her face at the toilet sink.

Almost an hour had passed since she had left her seat. The train would soon be arriving at Southampton station. Thankful that her seat had not been taken and that her luggage was still in place, she sat down.

*Get a grip, Prince!*

# Chapter 2

Sarah had at long last managed to get a good night's sleep aboard the *Coral Queen*. The ship docked at 5.30am, but she was woken by her alarm clock half an hour before.

*Here goes.* She heaved herself out of bed and groaned. Turnaround days were the busiest for crew members who had to make sure that all passengers disembarked, dealing with around 9,000 pieces of luggage, and then ready the ship for the new arrivals. The *Coral Queen* was one of the larger vessels on the oceans, carrying 3,500 passengers and 1,800 crew members, and she would be heading to the Mediterranean later that day.

The busiest crew members would be the stateroom stewards, of course, as they had to clean all of the passenger cabins thoroughly and have them ready for the new passengers in just a few hours. In addition to this, the whole ship had to be cleaned inside and out. Their work was checked by Heinz Linz, the Hotel Manager, who was meticulous with his inspections. The stateroom stewards knew that if he found one piece of dirt or debris, he would be down on them like a ton of bricks.

A knock at the door grabbed Sarah's attention. On opening it, she saw her friend and colleague, Brigitte.

"You look ready to roll." Sarah observed that Brigitte was dressed in shorts and t-shirt.

"I am. Can you believe it, I have never been to London?" Her French accent revealed her nationality.

"Well, enjoy yourself and I'll catch you later," said Sarah. "Make sure you do the London Eye."

"Top of my list," Brigitte called as she was already halfway down the corridor. "Missing you already."

"Yeah, really?" Sarah closed the door.

Turnaround was not such a bad day for the nurses, who had to restock the medical rooms and ensure that no drugs would go out of date during the next fourteen-night cruise, as well as collect health questionnaires in the passenger lounge. Janice had already placed the order for new supplies. Brigitte was taking the day off and heading to London for a few hours to see the sights on one of the tour buses. Passengers who were staying on board for back-to-back cruises were also given the option of a London tour.

Sarah and Bernard, a Philippine male nurse, were scheduled to be in the passenger lounge later, collecting questionnaires about recent vomiting or diarrhoea from the passengers. Sarah had discovered that seasoned cruisers did not admit to any such illness, knowing that they would be confined to their stateroom for a few days if they did. She hated telling new cruisers, who were just being honest, that their first few days would be limited to their rooms. It was a necessary precaution, however, because the Norovirus (Norwalk) could spread around a ship like a wildfire and ruin everyone's holiday. Medical and nursing staff would be called out *ad infinitum* to attend to every passenger or crew member who had picked it up.

Sarah had only encountered one episode of Norovirus early on in her cruising experience, and luckily the medics had managed to contain the outbreak in one small part of the ship. The *Coral Queen* boasted a high standard of hygiene, but buffets were lethal if this marauder invaded.

*I would ban buffets altogether if it was left to me.* Sarah knew that the restaurant and buffet staff did their best to ensure that passengers used hand gels on entering any dining area, but there were always a stubborn few who snubbed them.

The Canary Islands cruise they had just been on had turned out to be excessively busy. Lots of sea days always meant busy times in the medical centre. Sarah had been on call for the past seventy-two hours and had been up most nights, attending to minor ailments and injuries. Many of the ailments were due to excessive drinking by both passengers and crew. The crew tended to let their hair down during their time off in the bar below the waterline. Sarah had ventured into the crew bar on rare occasions, but it was not for the fainthearted.

"It's like a viper's nest down there," Janice, the senior nurse warned her when she first joined ship, but at least one visit to the bar was a necessary initiation for Sarah so that she knew what to expect during on-call hours.

Sarah had noticed that most nationalities tended to group together with their own countrymen. Seating was scarce in the crew bar whereas alcohol was abundantly available. During her very first cruise, she was having a drink with Bernard when a fight had broken out between a Romanian and a Russian, and it didn't end well.

Crowds gathered round as it turned nasty.

"So much for a quiet night," Bernard moaned, holding Sarah back. "Wait for security or you might end up hurt."

Security arrived and pulled the men apart. Sarah could see there was blood everywhere. She had spent the night helping the doctor to stitch the Romanian man's face. He'd ended up with stitches that ran from above his left eye down to his chin due to an injury sustained from a broken bottle.

Bernard had dealt with the Russian kitchen worker, who'd suffered a broken nose and had two front teeth knocked out.

"He was ugly before, now he's grotesque," Bernard whispered to her afterwards.

"You're incorrigible," Sarah replied.

"Serves him right for ruining my down-time."

"What happens to them now?" Sarah had asked Janice.

"Security are here to collect them. They will be locked up and thrown off ship at the next port without any fare home."

Discipline on board a ship had to be strict otherwise rival factions could create chaos. The crew knew the consequences of serious misdemeanours. Sarah understood the need, but couldn't help feeling sorry for the two men, knowing they would have very little money when they were escorted off the ship.

"There is a no tolerance policy towards this kind of violence," Janice explained.

Other drink-related mishaps commonly involved passengers with drinks packages and those who sneaked liquor on board. These passengers also accounted for many of the night-time call-outs. Occasionally there would be passengers or crew members who had taken drugs. Sarah had been surprised to discover that passengers could be locked up for drugs offences if security felt it necessary, but it was uncommon. Crew had to undergo regular drugs tests, and any who tested positive were also chucked off ship at the next port.

Sarah was thankful there had been no serious illnesses or injuries during the latest cruise. In general, both crew and passengers had been happy – barring a few disgruntled passengers who would never be satisfied. She smiled as she thought of how nice it would be not to have to see Mr Bragen ever again. Mr Bragen had been a passenger with a chronic leg ulcer who, in spite of having his own attending private nurse, insisted on turning up to one of the surgeries held twice daily to have his dressings checked. She would hear him before she saw him: a loud and uncouth man who always demanded to be seen straight away.

"No, I will not take a seat. Where's my nurse?"

Sarah would cringe before straightening up and heading out to the waiting area.

"Mr Bragen, please come through. What a pleasure it is to see you again."

"Like hell it is. Let's just get on with it and none of your British charm. I'm immune."

*I couldn't agree more, and thankfully not all Americans are like you!*

"As you wish." She would smile at Delia, his private nurse whom she had got to know quite well, as she wheeled him into the surgery.

"How do you put up with him?" she had asked privately. Delia had sniggered.

"I have very thick skin, and for the money he pays, I would do almost anything."

Delia helped Sarah to deal with this rude man, and she was right – he paid well and left generous tips. He even gave Sarah a gold brooch. She would have refused it, but he had sneaked it onto her desk while she wasn't looking, along with a *thank-you* card, on the last day. By then, she was too busy to track him down to return it.

*Anyway, no more Mr Bragen. I can't wait to see Rachel today.*

Sarah was three months into a nine-month contract with Queen Cruises, and she had finally got used to the shifts and facilities available aboard ship. It had taken a while to adjust from hospital life to that of a nurse on a cruise ship, but she enjoyed the work and managed to get some time off when the ship was in port. In many ways, working on a cruise ship beat hospitals on land. Time off was shared between herself, Bernard, Brigitte and Janice. The doctors also shared time off between themselves. As long as there was a doctor and two nurses on duty when the ship was in port, the others could go on land. Other than that, they were never really off duty because they had to respond to emergencies night and day.

Sarah had saved up quite a bit of time off so that she would be able to spend time with Rachel. Bernard and Brigitte had been happy to take extra trips on the Canaries cruise when she had explained Rachel would be travelling alone.

"Poor girl," said Brigitte. "Men are scum." She did a pretend spitting motion.

"Hey – am I invisible?" Bernard protested.

"You are not, but you should be." Sarah nudged him playfully. Bernard was in fact happily married with two children back home in Manila. "Poor Rachel, she has had a horrid time. She was absolutely besotted with the man."

"As you can't bring yourself to say his name, I take it you didn't like him," Brigitte observed.

"To be honest, I never took to *Robert*." Sarah said the name pointedly. "Obviously, even if I had liked him, I wouldn't now, but he completely took over Rachel's life. Right from the start, he took her away from everything and everyone that she knew."

"Controlling then?" asked Bernard.

"Yes, it was subtle at first, but I recognised his controlling nature early on. The signs were there, but it was impossible to broach the subject with Rachel. Even when she phoned, he always seemed to be there. It was as if she wasn't allowed to speak without his permission. I was going to try to talk to Rachel about it, but I chickened out. She was so happy and I didn't want to make her sad."

"Perhaps as well, else she might not have been able to face you now when she needs you," said Brigitte.

"You're right, but I had already decided it was Rachel's choice, and I was going to try to like the man."

Sarah couldn't help thinking that Rachel was better off without him, but knew that it would take some time for her to recover from the breakup.

"As I said, men are scum." Brigitte folded her arms and glared at Bernard, who smirked.

"She's a fitness fanatic, so I'm just hoping that she enjoys the cruise and I have done the right thing persuading her to join me, especially as our time together will be limited. But it's got to be better than working all hours, which is the way that Rachel has been dealing with it."

"Don't worry, we will cover for you as much as possible. Anything to help a damsel in distress." Bernard turned to Brigitte. "As you see, not all men are scum."

That conversation had been a few days ago. Sarah was pleased that she worked with great people even though change was on the horizon.

Once Sarah was washed and dressed in her passenger deck officer uniform, she was ready for the day. She smiled to herself as she looked at the four different uniforms in her wardrobe.

"You have four uniforms to be worn on different occasions, and woe betide you if you get it wrong." Janice had given her a tour on her first day and then showed her to her living quarters. "There is a day uniform to be worn in passenger areas and a night uniform for the same areas. You can wear scrubs during surgery hours and when in the medical centre, and for formal nights you wear this baby." Janice held up yet another white starched uniform that was even more pristine than the others.

"I will do my best to comply," Sarah had answered, but what had seemed very confusing then was now second nature to her. As a nurse, she had officer status and proudly boasted two-and-a-half gold stripes on her epaulettes.

After putting on the day uniform, she made her way two doors down to see Janice. Janice had been senior nurse on the ship for a year, but she was moving to another ship after a short break to see her parents in Scotland. Sarah had been trained by Janice, and in spite of a fifteen-year age difference, they had become good friends.

Janice opened the door dressed casually in beige cotton trousers and the t-shirt Sarah had bought her as a leaving present. The bright yellow letters spoke volumes: 'LIFE IS FOR LIVING'.

"You'll never believe it, I slept in!" Janice exclaimed. "Thankfully, I packed last night so I'm ready to go."

"I'm going to miss you," said Sarah, to which Janice smiled.

"You'll be fine. You never know, you might get someone your own age to talk to."

"And I might get a dragon!" Sarah smiled wistfully, although she was not one to be negative. They hugged briefly, and then Janice turned to grab her hand luggage as her suitcase had been collected the night before and would be waiting for her in the baggage hall on the dockside.

"Good luck, Sarah, and enjoy yourself with your friend. I'd better get going before they keep me on board."

They walked together towards the lifts and hugged before Sarah took the stairs to the medical centre. Janice wasn't the only one leaving today. Marek, the junior doctor (or 'baby doc' as junior doctors are known on board a cruise ship), had completed his contract and decided that ship medicine wasn't for him. He missed his girlfriend, a ward sister at St Thomas's Hospital in London, so he had managed to get a job as a locum GP in Hackney. He was hoping to 'pop the question' as soon as he got to London.

Dr Graham Bentley would be staying, which was a good thing because he was so experienced in ship medicine and brilliant in an emergency. Dr Bentley was the chief medical officer and the first in command of the medical team.

It had taken Sarah a while to get used to the cruise-line hierarchy at first. The chief generally saw passengers and the baby doc was responsible for the health of the crew. The nurses saw both passengers and crew members, with the senior nurse ensuring everything ran smoothly and that passengers were billed appropriately.

Bernard and Brigitte were also staying, so at least Sarah could still have a laugh. They had similar senses of humour – humour that only nurses could share.

Among the many other staff moving on today, the one that was hardest for Sarah to take was Barry. The engineering officer was being moved to join the same ship as Janice. Sarah and Barry had got on from the first time they met and had become good friends. His impending move was one of the things that had stopped them becoming a couple; that and the small matter of his being engaged to the assistant cruise director on the ship he was soon to be joining. Sarah had fought off her feelings and Barry's advances, determined not to do to someone else what had been done to Rachel and having a stubborn belief in right and wrong. Her faith had taken a battering over the past five years, but although she no longer went to church, she still had a strong moral code that she couldn't quite shake off.

"It's perhaps as well he is leaving – it could only have ended badly." Bernard had comforted her the night before by helping her to avoid a long goodbye. Barry had made it obvious Bernard wasn't welcome, but at Sarah's request, he had stuck to her like glue, and Barry had finally given up.

Sarah knew that the long hours and the close proximity of other crew members resulted in multiple casual relationships on board. For some girls, it was their first time away from home, and they equated the freedom that came with it with being free to sleep around. It didn't always go to plan as the men often promised much and delivered little. Some of these relationships even ended up in crew presenting with venereal diseases. There was one crew member who attended surgery regularly for antibiotics, and no matter how much Sarah and the doctors tried to advise him to practise safe sex, he just didn't get it.

"Why should I? I can get treatment when I need it."

Marek had threatened not to treat him the next time, but they all knew that a doctor couldn't withhold the treatment, if only for the sakes of the girls that he slept with.

"One day you will have a resistant strain of the disease and then I won't be able to treat you. When that happens, you will be sacked to safeguard the rest of the crew."

Sarah took a deep breath as she unlocked the door and entered the medical centre.

# Chapter 3

"It seems to be taking an inordinately long time to get there." Marjorie knew the journey from London to Southampton was only about seventy miles. She hadn't really been taking much notice of the road, but now she looked out of the window, she could see that the M3 was virtually at a standstill going north. Although she was travelling south, the car was going very slowly.

"What's happening, Johnson?" she asked the chauffer of the white Rolls Royce they were travelling in.

"We passed an accident a while back, ma'am, but we're almost at our turnoff. We have plenty of time."

Johnson hesitated as if he wanted to say something.

"Is there something else, Johnson?"

"You seem to be worried about something ma'am. Are you sure that you should take this trip alone? You have only just got over the accident and Lord Snellthorpe trusted me to look after you."

"You know that Ralph and I loved cruising and he would have wanted me to carry on." She wiped a tear away from her face. "I will be fine on board the *Coral*

*Queen*. The staff will look after me and I have plenty of books to keep me occupied."

"Yes, I'm sure they will, madam."

Lady Snellthorpe was touched by Johnson's concern for her welfare. Her maid had told her that he had tried to get tickets for the cruise but found it was fully booked. The maid said Johnson had checked the day before, deciding to spend the money left to him by Lord Snellthorpe on the cruise, so that he'd keep an eye on her from a distance.

The nagging feeling returned.

Marjorie Snellthorpe was deep in thought. She hardly ever travelled in the Rolls, but the Bentley was in the garage having a re-spray following her minor bump the previous week. Her mind wandered back to that event. She had decided to go shopping on her own, much to the dismay of her housekeeper, Mrs Ratton. A car had crashed into the side of hers as she was turning a corner. The driver had seemingly come from nowhere, and when they collided, he stared at her menacingly. As he appeared to be getting out of the car, her first thought was that she was about to be a victim of road-rage, but a woman had come to her assistance. The driver had jumped back into his car and driven off at speed.

It had been traumatic, and when the police came, Marjorie had been unable to give them much information. She could remember the face of the driver, but nothing about the car, other than that is was possibly grey. The police had been sympathetic but unable to take it any further, and she had agreed that they were unlikely to be able to track the driver down.

She shuddered as she thought of the accident, still uncertain whether it had been deliberate. Marjorie had not thought so initially, but as she remembered how it had occurred and how intimidating the man had looked, a nagging feeling that it was not an accident wormed its way into her mind.

She had shared her concerns with her son, Jeremy, but he'd scoffed at her as he always did.

"Don't be ridiculous, Mother, you have been watching too much American television," he shouted. He always seemed to shout these days. "Why would anyone want to crash into you on purpose?"

"Why indeed? I'm sure you're right, Jeremy, perhaps I get a little over anxious since your father died. I miss him terribly."

Her son had changed the subject all too quickly and asked her for yet another injection of cash into the family business.

"Jeremy, you have had three large sums of money in the past twelve months. Why do you need more?"

She could see that her son was fighting to control his temper. He had always hated being challenged, but since taking over the management of the business, he had become overly quick to fly off the handle.

"Mother, you don't understand business. These are difficult times and we need to keep competitive."

"We're not in trouble, are we?" Marjorie was worried. Although she didn't understand the business, she did understand money management, and Ralph had always warned her about Jeremy's spending habits. She hoped rather than believed that the money was going into the business as she signed the cheque.

"Of course not. You just don't understand what it needs. Dad left it in a right mess."

Jeremy snatched the cheque. Marjorie didn't believe for a moment that this was true, but knew the pointlessness of trying to speak to her son when he was in that sort of mood.

"Oh well, Randolph and Philip are going to bring me in to explain the business and accounting side of things when I get back from my cruise, so I should understand it better then."

Randolph was the family lawyer and remained as loyal to Marjorie as he had been to her husband. He had called the previous week to say that he needed to speak with her and explain some things about the business, but that she should go and enjoy her holiday first. It could wait until she returned. Philip Mason was financial director of the company and a close friend of Ralph's. Randolph had explained he wanted Philip to be present at the meeting.

"I don't know why he feels the need to get you involved. I am managing things perfectly well. You have to trust me, Mother."

Before she had time to think about her reply, Jeremy had gone. The sadness of having a son who didn't seem to care about her returned, but it made her determined to do what Ralph would have wanted. Jeremy would just have to lump it. She feared it would not be good news awaiting her on her return, but she decided to try not to think about it too much until then.

The car stopped and she could see that they were at the cruise terminal. It looked busy, and for a brief moment, Marjorie wondered if Johnson might have been right about her travelling on her own.

*It's too late now.* She straightened up as Johnson opened the door to let her out.

# Chapter 4

At long last, the train arrived in Southampton, and people were making a dash for the doors as if their lives depended on it. The elderly man who had been sitting next to Rachel had got off a stop earlier. Phone-girl and her boyfriend had gathered their things and gone to block the corridor, along with all the other people who hadn't yet wound down into holiday mode.

Rachel remained seated. It wasn't as if people needed to hurry as the train terminated here. She had plenty of time to get to the cruise terminal, and having attended far too many crowd-control events, she was happy to let the crowds disperse. She did keep one eye on her suitcase, though, just to be sure that it didn't leave without her.

After about five minutes, it was safe to get up and walk to her luggage without being crammed up against people. She noticed that a few other people had had the same idea and were casually gathering their things together, too.

She collected her suitcase and negotiated her way on to the platform, pausing to ensure that her hand luggage and handbag were securely in place before extending the suitcase handle and wheeling it along the platform towards the ticket barrier. She couldn't resist smiling as she noticed phone-girl and her partner, stuck in a queue at a different ticket barrier. Phone-girl was now chewing gum with mouth wide open and blowing bubbles.

*Not a great look.*

Once outside, Rachel joined the taxi queue. It appeared that the majority of people were heading to the cruise terminals with three sailings taking place today, so she heard a man in front say. After about twenty minutes of waiting, she got into a taxi and asked the driver to take her to the Mayflower Terminal where the *Coral Queen* would be berthed.

"You going on a cruise then?" he asked.

"Yes, I am."

"Where are you going?"

"Around the Med," Rachel replied. "I'm meeting a friend who works as a nurse on the ship."

"Oh, you'll get to see *Upstairs, Downstairs* then." The taxi driver laughed.

"Yes, I suppose I will. I hadn't thought of that." Rachel joined in and laughed for the first time that day, relaxing. She even started to feel a little bit excited.

"You'll see the ships any minute."

Just as he said that, she saw the enormous cruise ships in the distance. They became bigger and bigger as the taxi got closer.

"Wow! I don't think I imagined they would be that big. Which one is the *Coral Queen*?"

"That one on the right. We just have to do a bit of a circle and then we will be there."

Once at the gate, the taxi driver held out a pass that was checked by a security guard and then he was allowed through. As they pulled up at what appeared to be the terminal, there were more queues of people. The driver pulled in to the side, getting out to open her door.

On opening the boot, the driver stood aside as the ship crew came to collect her suitcase. After checking the label, they put it on a luggage crate and it was taken away. Rachel paid the taxi driver and walked towards the crowds that were heading inside the terminal.

"Bye, love, have a nice holiday," shouted the taxi driver and Rachel waved.

"Thanks, I think I will."

Once inside the terminal, she showed her ticket to a security guard at the bottom of an escalator.

"Go up to the next floor where you can check in and pass through customs."

The man stood aside. Once at the top, Rachel joined a long queue which was organised by makeshift barriers into the shape of a snake. She counted twelve desks at the end of the queue where people were checking in.

While standing in the queue, Rachel noticed people passing through on the right-hand side to two VIP desks where they were immediately checked in. She saw an elderly lady being pushed in a wheelchair by a uniformed chauffeur. The lady had beautiful white hair and was well-dressed in a fine silk dress with a white cotton jacket. Once at the desk, she was greeted warmly by the staff and taken through by one of the volunteers that Rachel had seen milling around. The chauffeur said goodbye and walked away, but then turned to watch. Rachel couldn't help but notice the look on his face as he watched the old lady go.

*I wonder what he's worried about.*

The queue started to move again, and she forgot about the old lady. Eventually, she arrived at one of the desks.

"Have you cruised before?" the lady at the desk asked.

"No I haven't," Rachel replied.

"Okay, I need to take a photo of you for your cruise card. The card will be your pass on and off the ship and also used for purchases while you're on board. I need to register a credit card to link it to."

Rachel handed over a credit card and signed a form permitting payment to be taken from her card at the end of the cruise.

"Look into the camera."

Rachel saw what looked like a web-cam. She was about to smile, but it flashed before she had the chance. She glanced at the photo on the screen that would be linked to the card. It made her look like one of her prisoners, but she wasn't that worried.

*After all, who will see it?*

She was then given a folded, cardboard map of the ship. Finally, she was handed a questionnaire to fill out in the departure lounge.

"Enjoy your cruise," said the lady. "Follow the crowds."

Next stop was security, and all her hand luggage was passed along a conveyor belt to be scanned. Rachel passed through a metal detector, and once given the all clear, she moved into an enormous room where people were being asked to wait until their key-card colour was called. She caught a glimpse of the elderly lady coming out of a lift at the top of the stairs and being wheeled towards the ship.

Rachel filled out the questionnaire relating to recent gastrointestinal upsets, of which she had had none. She looked around at her fellow passengers and was not surprised that there were lots of young people and families. Sarah had explained that cruises were likely to be taken by anyone now, and not just the elderly rich.

*I guess we are all much better off than we used to be*, thought Rachel. She had recently had a pay rise herself when she qualified as a police constable. *WPC Prince,* she thought proudly, finally allowing some self-satisfaction to surface. She had spent so much time being maudlin and was ready to allow a little bit of joy back into her life, deciding right then and there that she would be the old Rachel again: the girl who loved life and had a great sense of humour.

It was time to put Robert in the past and get on with her life.

She felt better already, and her excitement mounted as she caught sight of Sarah collecting questionnaires. Sarah and Rachel had been friends since schooldays. They had lived two blocks away from each other, gone to the same church where Rachel's dad was the vicar, and ended up at the same university in Leeds. Sarah had studied for a nursing degree while Rachel studied history. They'd shared the flat where Rachel still lived from the second year of their student days, but Sarah had tired of hospital life and decided she wanted to travel.

Rachel had graduated with a first-class honours degree in history, but she hadn't known what she wanted to do for a career when she started the course. Initially, she thought about teaching, but one term in a secondary school convinced her it wasn't for her. In spite of her father's occupation, she had never considered pursuing theology, and her parents had always allowed her to choose what she wanted to do with her life. They had never pushed religion down her throat, either; she had realised for herself that she believed in God from an early age.

It was an incident that had occurred in her first year at university that sparked her interest in becoming a police officer, and her ultimate dream now was to become a detective and join the intelligence services. One day while studying in the shared sitting room at university, she'd heard a group of students come in. Some were speaking Arabic, and some were speaking in English. There had been recent terrorist attacks in France and Belgium, and she could hear that they were having a heated argument about them. They were not aware of her presence because she was sitting in a high-backed chair in a corner of the room – she had chosen the spot deliberately to do some studying.

While she couldn't understand a lot of the conversation because the students kept switching languages, she could hear that a couple of the boys and one girl were saying how awful the terrorist attacks were and that it went against Islam. However, a boy who sounded older than the others shouted them down, and whatever he said, they seemed afraid to challenge him. She heard words like 'holy war', 'infidels', and that the West was full of immoral people.

"LOOK AT HOW THE WOMEN DRESS!" he shouted. "They have no shame."

"It's a different culture," said another male voice. "We should not judge, Allah would not want us to judge."

"You are only saying that because you have been sucked in by their ways," one of the girls replied. "I have seen you hanging around with Bethany."

More Arabic shouting followed, and then Rachel heard some of them leave. Shocked by the parts of the conversation that she had understood, she took a peep around the chair to see if she recognised any of the remaining students. She was horrified to see that the man who had been doing all the shouting was Mohab from one of her history classes. She had spoken to him a few times during a study group and he'd seemed mild-mannered, even if he was a bit aloof.

One of the boys turned his head to check if anyone was in the room and she just managed to duck back behind the chair in time. She could feel her heart pounding; she felt frightened.

*What will they do if they realise I am here?*

She tried to convince herself that it was a free country and they were just having a political argument like many students do. Certainly, nothing she had heard gave any impression that they were plotting anything or that they would be likely to do so. Should she go to the police? What would she say if she did? That a group of students were discussing events that had occurred and were arguing about it – these sorts of arguments occurred in universities all of the time. In her history class, a few people stated they were republican and they would like to see the monarchy removed. It didn't mean that they intended to march on Buckingham Palace and kill the Queen! She reasoned that she needed to keep the conversation she had overheard in perspective; she didn't even know who the students were, apart from Mohab.

Later that night, Rachel had discussed it with Sarah, and although she'd agreed the conversation was disturbing, she'd also agreed that people were entitled to their views and no threats had been made.

"The only thing I can suggest is that you report Mohab to the anti-hate crime hotline to make them aware of his extremist views."

"Yes, good idea. I would never forgive myself if he turned out to be dangerous, and I hadn't done anything." Mohab's aggression and dominance had unnerved Rachel, even though some of the group had disagreed with him. She reported what she had heard, and as far as she was concerned, that was the end of the matter.

She had watched Mohab more carefully during the classes they shared, sitting a few rows back from him to see how he behaved. He behaved normally in classes and was respectful to the lecturers and other students, but occasionally she noticed a glimpse of anger in his eyes when certain girls entered the room, particularly Muslim girls who chose not to wear the hijab. Rachel knew some Christian men felt the same way about how girls from their churches dressed and behaved, so this alone was not a major cause for concern. Her own father had often had to calm down the more dogmatic members of his congregation.

About six weeks after the sitting room event, Rachel was returning to her halls of residence after a class when she noticed Mohab having a particularly heated argument with two boys. She saw two men approach him, show him a card, handcuff him and march him away. The boys he had been arguing with actually looked pleased and she wondered whether they too had reported him to the authorities.

It was at that moment she realised that she may have prevented a serious crime, and she knew what she wanted to do with her life. As soon as she finished her degree, she applied to the police force, and after passing the rigorous selection process, she was offered a trainee constable position.

# Chapter 5

Sarah had agreed to meet Bernard in the medical centre before going off ship. The medical centre consisted of a passenger waiting area, two clinic rooms, a treatment room, an office and a clinical store. During a cruise, two surgeries were held for passengers and staff, one in the morning and one in the evening.

One member of the medical team held the emergency bleep at all times. When on call, they had to lug around a large suitcase on wheels which contained emergency equipment for any eventuality. Sarah had found this stressful initially, but once she had got used to the layout of the ship and discovered the quickest routes to any given area on board, it became easier. The most difficult places to access were those below the waterline as conditions were cramped. Engineering was the worst as the space was really tight.

"Hello, darling," Bernard greeted Sarah as she arrived. "We were just having coffee."

Sarah could see that Bernard was relaxing with Dr Graham Bentley while they had the opportunity. She poured herself a mug of filter coffee from the steel jug which had been sent up from the kitchens and joined them.

"I will be with the captain later so I will leave it to you two to welcome our new team members," Graham said. "The senior nurse is Australian and has worked on cruise ships for another cruise line, so you will need to brief her on how this girl runs. Her name is Gwen Sumner."

"Don't you worry, sir, we will sort her out," said Bernard with a mischievous glint in his eye.

"Mm, I will rely on you to be the sensible one, Sarah," continued Graham. "The new baby doc is called Alessandro Romano. He's Italian and has been working in refugee camps in the Middle East for a year. Before that, he worked in emergency care for a hospital in Rome so he should be able to cope. He may need guiding with medication names, but thankfully you two can prescribe and Brigitte is used to foreign sounding meds."

"It's as well he will be dealing with more crew than passengers. Some of our wealthier visitors might be too much of a culture shock after refugee camps," said Sarah sympathetically. "Come on, Bernard, time to go."

"Okay, you're in charge, Doctor," Bernard teased as they left the medical centre.

"I'll get you back for that one later," retorted Graham. He was happy to banter, but everyone knew who was in charge when leadership was required.

Sarah and Bernard left the ship, passing through security, and made their way down to the passenger waiting areas. The VIPs and people requiring assistance from volunteers were allowed to board immediately, and only if they had given a positive answer to the diarrhoea and vomiting question were they detained, so most of the action took place in the main waiting area.

Passengers were called through in order of the decks they were to be staying on. Sarah and Bernard collected the questionnaires as they queued to pass through security. It was a tedious job, but it had to be done in order to protect both passengers and crew from the unpleasant virus. As this was a summer cruise, the likelihood of norovirus was much lower than during the winter, but Graham would not be happy if they missed a potential outbreak.

"Oh, I can see Rachel," said Sarah.

"Where?" Bernard asked as he continued to keep one eye on the questionnaires being handed to him.

"Over there, in the pink t-shirt and jeans. There's a pink polka-dot suitcase next to her."

"You didn't tell me she was beautiful," said Bernard admiringly. "So sad she has a broken heart."

"She'll be alright." Sarah looked at her friend and saw that Bernard was quite right. Rachel was perfectly proportioned with long blonde hair, and she really was stunning.

"I hope so. She's far too beautiful to become a wallflower."

"Now the queue has died down, do you mind if I go and say hello?"

"Go ahead, I'll call you if anyone collapses," said Bernard, laughing.

Rachel had already spotted Sarah, and the women jumped up and down with excitement as they embraced.

"It's wonderful to see you, Rachel."

"You too, you look great. Obviously, life on the high seas is suiting you."

"You look good, too. I can't wait to show you around. I'll catch up with you after the safety drill tonight. What time are you eating?"

"I chose 6.30pm dining so that I could take in some shows and the gym afterwards," said Rachel.

"Trust you! What stateroom are you in?"

"I'm on deck nine – room 9003."

"Great, I'll catch you later. Your stateroom is on the starboard side at the front of the ship. I'd better get back to work."

Some of the other passengers smiled as Sarah left her friend.

A man sitting on the other side of the room had also been admiring Rachel's looks from afar.

*Maybe when the job's done, I can have some leisure time with that one,* he thought. He was a bit disappointed to see the woman in uniform arrive on the scene.

*Perhaps as well I know she has a friend on the crew. I can't afford to draw attention to myself.*

# Chapter 6

Rachel headed towards the crowds as she heard her deck number called out and joined a line of people for a relatively long walk upwards via makeshift ramps. There had been a bottleneck at the beginning as people were being urged by the ship's photographers to have a pre-cruise photo taken, but Rachel had taken the opportunity to bypass it while a large family was being directed into position. After that, the walk was relatively simple. As she arrived at the entrance to the ship, her photo pass was scanned and she was on board the *Coral Queen*.

Waiters were handing out champagne or soft drinks to passengers on their arrival, and Rachel noted a few sales desks out to nab passengers as they boarded. Sarah had warned her about how expensive things could be on the ship. Rachel had been given a drinks package as part of her booking, meaning she would be able to choose from a limited range of wines or spirits and all soft drinks without extra cost.

She realised she was in the upper part of the ship's atrium and was struck by its opulence. The atrium spanned two decks and there were seats and pristine, shining tables scattered around. She could see a number of eating areas including a patisserie, a pizza lounge and a few coffee bars on the deck below.

She found herself a seat and noticed the old lady from the VIP entrance sitting with a glass of champagne, but not drinking it. The lady looked troubled. Rachel's instinct was telling her that something was not right, but her deliberating over whether to go and join her ended when a man and woman, who looked to be in their fifties, approached. The woman was incredibly well-dressed for a boarding day, wearing a blue silk dress with a laced V-neck.

"Are these seats taken?" the man asked in an American drawl.

"No, help yourself." Rachel smiled.

"Are you travelling alone, dear?" asked the woman.

*Get right to it why don't you?*

"Yes and no," Rachel replied. "I have a friend who works on board and she will be joining me for some of my trips. Where are you from?"

"We're from New York City, ma'am," said the man. "We take regular cruises and this is about our third around the Mediterranean. Rome is by far my favourite place. Isn't that right, Mildred? I'm Joe, this is Mildred. Do you have a name?"

"How do you do, Joe and Mildred. I am Rachel and my friend is called Sarah. She is one of the ship's nurses."

"Well hopefully we won't be meeting her in her professional capacity," said Mildred, laughing.

Joe chatted away, making easy conversation, and Rachel was happy to listen as she didn't want him to ask her what she did. She had debated whether she should tell a white lie while she was on board the *Coral Queen* and say she was a civil servant rather than a policewoman, mainly because she did not want to hear the inevitable "Evening all" jokes or stories about criminal relatives (or indeed anything work-related). She needn't have worried in this instance, though, as Joe and Mildred were happy to talk about themselves.

The announcement came over the ship's loudspeaker that passengers could go to their staterooms and Rachel excused herself. She noted she was currently on deck five and her cabin was on deck nine – *I must get used to calling it a stateroom*. When she had asked Joe and Mildred about cabins, they had been shocked.

"They're called staterooms, dear," Mildred had explained. "They are far grander than any cabins I have ever seen."

The lifts were packed with people, and even though there were six of them where she was standing, Rachel decided to run up the stairs. She had not done any exercise at all today, and she usually took in a morning run and an evening gym session. Having noticed a number of well-proportioned people milling around, she was determined not to gain weight over the next fortnight.

*Cruise or no cruise, I will keep fit.*

The stairs were wide with shiny banisters that had obviously been freshly polished. They rose in sections that enabled them to spiral up through the central area between the lifts. Rachel gulped in air when she arrived on deck nine, but felt stimulated by the exertion.

Large bronze plaques were on the wall with odd room numbers on one side and even on the other. Rachel hadn't yet worked out which side was starboard and which was port. She knew that starboard was right and port was left when facing the front, but she didn't know which way was the front.

Once she had worked out which side of the ship, the odd numbers were on and the direction her room was in, she stepped into the corridor.

*Gosh, I knew it was big, but this corridor must be a mile long.* There were lots of people walking up and down a fairly narrow corridor and she had to step into indents where cabins – *whoops, staterooms* – were to let people pass who had a lot more hand luggage than she was carrying. She noticed that luggage was also starting to appear outside some of the staterooms and she passed a room with a 'do not disturb' sign on the outside.

Room 9003 was almost at the end of the corridor, a fair walk from where she had exited the stairs at midships. She noticed another lift area nearer to her stateroom and assumed there would be more towards the rear of the ship.

As she was making her way forward, she saw the old lady she had spotted earlier walking slowly along the corridor, dragging her hand luggage along behind her.

"Can I help you with that?" Rachel asked.

"No thank you, dear, I have already turned down one of the stewards, and he might be offended if he sees me accepting help from someone else. Although I'm beginning to wish I had taken him up on his offer."

The old lady smiled, and the worry appeared to leave her for the moment. Although she looked frail, her eyes were sharp, and Rachel suspected that she was a 'no-nonsense' type of woman.

"Where are you heading?" Rachel asked.

The lady looked confused for a moment, then checked her papers and answered, "I am in 9005."

"I think we will be neighbours then," said Rachel. "I was told midships was the more comfortable."

*Tactless,* she thought, slightly embarrassed. She had noticed the lady earlier passing through the VIP lounge and presumed she could afford the more expensive rooms.

"I thought I would try out a different part of the ship for a change," replied the old lady. Her eyes misted up momentarily before she blinked and came back to the present. "What about you? Is this your first cruise?"

"Yes." *Is cruise virgin stamped on my forehead?* "A friend invited me. She works on the ship as a nurse and decided I needed a holiday."

"How nice, I do hope you will enjoy yourself. Cruises can be great fun. I have done fifteen on this cruise line, which in my opinion is the best. This is my first one alone." Her eyes became sad again. "My name is Marjorie."

"I'm Rachel. My friend is called Sarah, but I'm not sure how much I will see of her. It depends how busy the medical centre is. I have brought plenty of books though."

They arrived at their staterooms and parted company. Rachel liked the old lady; she definitely had breeding, and Rachel didn't believe she normally roughed it – if having a balcony room at the front of a ship could be considered roughing it. Not the prying type, either, which Rachel liked - and needed.

*Interested, but not nosey*, she thought, wondering again whether something was troubling her new neighbour.

# Chapter 7

Marjorie walked into her stateroom and saw that the double bed had been made up. Not for the first time, she wondered whether this whole cruise idea had been a mistake.

*There's still time to leave the ship.*

She had never felt so alone. For sixty years, she had been married to her beloved husband, and although she had good friends, she knew that she would have to face some tough decisions over the next few months that she couldn't discuss with them.

Her mind wandered to her only son who appeared so cold these days.

*Where did we go wrong?* She asked herself this question for the thousandth time, but knew that she and her husband had not made Jeremy who he was. She so wanted to be able to confide in him; she had wanted to cry on his shoulder following his father's death, but he had seemed detached both before and after the funeral. She only saw him when he needed money for the business that her husband had worked his fingers to the bone to build.

The rumblings from the directors had made their way to her ears, but Marjorie had remained loyal to her son for months, explaining that it was early days and he would become more like his father in time. In her heart of hearts, she knew that this was never likely to happen. Her husband had managed to rein him in, but now that he was gone, Jeremy was left to do things the way he wanted. He had always been a bit like a bull in a china shop, never having the sensitivities required for managing people in the way that his father had.

*Perhaps we let him get away with too much when he was young.*

Their only child had been born out of a difficult pregnancy and an even more difficult labour. Marjorie's blood-pressure had been raised during her pregnancy and she had been confined to her home for the majority of the time. Labour came one awful, stormy night – as if it had been a sign of things to come. She had awoken with terrible pain and was taken to hospital where she spent the next forty hours in labour. When the time for delivery came, it was long and protracted, and in the end the doctor was called in by the midwife to carry out a forceps delivery.

Marjorie could still remember the excruciating pain as the local anaesthetic hadn't worked. Eventually, their son had been pulled out, screaming at the top of his voice.

"You have a baby boy!" the doctor had announced, happily. She'd held out her arms to take her baby, but he'd been put into a cot by the midwife and wrapped in a shawl.

After this, Marjorie had bled, and she could see the concern on the doctor's face as he tried to stem the bleeding. She remembered staring at the ceiling, crying out for her husband, who wasn't allowed in the room, and she sobbed at the thought that she would be facing death alone. All the time, she could hear a screaming baby.

"Please let me hold my son."

She'd pleaded, but the midwife was too busy rushing around handing the doctor bits of equipment to try to stem the bleeding. A blood transfusion was put up. Eventually, Marjorie had been taken to theatre for an operation to stop the blood loss. She had woken in the early hours of the next morning and seen Ralph's head resting on her bed.

"Thank God!" he'd said as he woke up. "I thought I'd lost you." The tears, that he had obviously been holding back, filled his eyes. "You are never going through that again."

She'd found out later that during the night-time operation, her womb had been removed to stop her from bleeding to death. Going through 'that' again would never be an option.

Marjorie's thoughts were interrupted by a knock at the stateroom door, which she had left ajar.

"Hello, madam, my name is Josie and I will be your stateroom attendant for this cruise." The voice was loud and jolly and came from a pint-sized Philippine lady. "Is there anything I can do for you at the moment, madam?"

Marjorie was well aware of how busy the room stewards were at this time. She and her husband had usually had a suite with a butler in attendance when they'd travelled together. Although she could still afford this type of room, she had always thought it an unnecessary extravagance, but Ralph had loved to treat her.

Realising that Josie was waiting for an answer, she lifted her head. "Not presently, thank you, but if you could ensure that there is a regular supply of Earl Grey and camomile tea in the room, I would be grateful."

"Absolutely, madam."

Marjorie surmised that Josie knew she was a VIP passenger and likely to be wealthy, so the attendant would go the extra mile. Stateroom stewards provided a good service to all of the guests, but there were those who left generous tips, usually Americans. Marjorie was also aware that Josie was more likely to receive a generous tip from those with plenty of money, and would be hoping she would oblige.

"If there is anything you need, just call housekeeping, madam, and I will do my best. There is an emergency drill at 5pm. Let me know if you need any assistance, ma'am."

"Thank you, Josie, but I am quite agile for my age!" She couldn't help but smile as Josie slipped into 'ma'am' and 'madam' at random.

"Oh, your luggage has arrived, madam. Bring it in here," Josie instructed a man twice her size. He obediently brought in the luggage and placed it carefully on the plastic sheet that lay over the foot of the bed for this purpose. With that, they both left the room.

Marjorie remained where she was and could hear Josie knocking at the door of the nice young lady she had met in the corridor.

*Rachel, I think her name was.*

# Chapter 8

Rachel checked out her room and appreciated its luxurious feel. She opened the balcony doors and stood on the balcony, enjoying the fresh air after travelling all day. She noticed the table and chairs that she could use for outdoor leisure and quiet times.

It was a pleasant day for England, but her room was facing the dockside so she couldn't watch any boats just yet. Instead, she watched men filling luggage trolleys and bringing them on board. She could also see what must be the bridge ahead of her as there were officers milling around in their white suits. It protruded out to the side as if floating in mid-air.

There was quite a bit of activity on the dockside as *Coral Queen* was due to sail at 4pm and it was now 3.30pm. She admired the well-oiled machine going on all around her and respected the efficiency.

Hearing a knock at the door, she went to answer it.

"Hello, madam. My name is Josie and I am your stateroom attendant for this cruise. Is everything to your satisfaction?" A very small woman with dark black hair was wearing a badge with her name on it over a maroon uniform.

"Everything's fine, thank you."

"Let me know if you need anything. Your luggage has arrived, madam. There will be an emergency drill at 5pm, madam."

"Please call me Rachel."

"Okay, madam Rachel," Josie replied, and off she bustled to the room next door.

Rachel chuckled as she brought in her suitcase and placed it on the bed so that she could unpack. This would all take some getting used to, but in the force, she called people sir and ma'am, so the situation was not entirely alien. She pulled in the suitcase and placed it on the bed so that she could unpack.

*I think I might enjoy this holiday after all.*

After unpacking, Rachel went upstairs to deck twelve. There a lively 'sailaway' party was rocking with music as people watched the ship manoeuvring through the Solent. A well-equipped deck confronted her with a large swimming pool, spa and children's pool along with a cocktail bar and a grill bar. Waiters strolled around offering cocktails to unsuspecting passengers, who were then asked to provide their stateroom card and sign a chit. All of these drinks would be added to the bill at the end of the cruise and could add up to a large sum over a two-week period.

"Don't take any cocktails off the waiters once you've had your free boarding champagne," Sarah had warned. "That's how the ship makes money when people first come on board – they think the drink is free, and once they realise it isn't, they are too embarrassed to refuse it. Stick to your drinks package allowance."

Rachel could see some people swimming already, and because of the hot summer afternoon, others had found sunbeds around the pool. A band played on a stage and the booming sound of the bass must have been audible from the dockside.

Rachel made her way to the side rails so that she could watch as the ship left Southampton. She couldn't believe how close some of the small sailing boats came, and every now and again, the ship would deliver a thunderous sound as the horn blasted to warn them to move away. A tiny dot of a motorboat with the word 'Pilot' on the side whose pilot had boarded to lead the ship safely out to sea before returning to port. Rachel looked forward to exploring the whole ship, but for now contented herself with watching people party and looking out to sea. The dock was becoming more and more distant as the ship moved away.

*How on earth do you navigate a ship this size through this busy port?* She admired the captain and the pilot immensely.

Rachel spotted a few passengers who she recognised from the departure lounge, including the man she had noticed watching her. He also seemed to be travelling alone. He was good-looking in a dark sort of way, with black cropped hair and a physique that made him look ex-military. Something about him made her feel uncomfortable. Maybe it was his good looks, or maybe it was because she was wary of men at the minute. The last thing she wanted was a man in her life.

Rachel texted her parents to let them know that she was safely aboard and would be out of range for a few days until they made the first port of Lisbon.

Her father texted back. *"Have a lovely holiday, we will miss you. Stay safe and give Sarah our love. Love you x"*

She was aware her parents worried about her since her engagement had broken off, and they had tried to support her as best they could.

*"Will do, Dad. Relaxing already, so looking forward to the cruise. Love to mum, see you when I get back xxx"*

The hour after departure passed quickly and soon the passengers were summoned to muster stations. Rachel attended the compulsory safety drill, which consisted of a lesson on the different alarm sounds and how to put on a lifejacket. The latter had been fun as some people needed assistance adjusting lifejackets to fit around generous waists and chests. Each lifejacket had a torch, and a whistle attached to it so passengers could be seen and heard in the dark. Fire safety was also covered as a fire on board a ship could be fatal. Some passengers were taking the drill a lot more seriously than others, but the crew were all taking it very seriously.

Rachel knew how important it could be for people to pay attention to a drill which might seem meaningless at the time. She herself had attended terror-attack and chemical-attack drills and she knew that the majority of people would not know how to react in such circumstances. Rachel paid the utmost attention to the safety drill, and by the end she knew how to put on her life jacket and how to find her muster station in the dark without using the lifts. Sarah would laugh at her because her nickname at university had been SWOT as opposed to SWAT. The man-overboard drill had been a sobering moment as she had recently read about a man who had gone missing while on a cruise. *Missing Presumed Dead*, the headline had read.

After about thirty minutes, the passengers were dismissed, and the atmosphere returned to holiday mode. Rachel made her way back to her stateroom so that she could change out of her travelling clothes and have a shower before dinner. She took the stairs down to deck four and made her way towards the restaurant.

It was huge. She could see the sheer scale of the room from where she stood in a queue that had formed. A crew member had already sprayed Rachel's hands with hand disinfectant while the Maître D' was welcoming everybody as they arrived. When she got to the desk, she had to look up as the Maître D' towered above her at around six foot six.

"What is your room number, madam?"

"It's 9003."

"Ah, Miss Prince. Are you happy to sit with others?"

"Yes, that would be fine."

"This will be your table for the rest of the cruise, madam. Welcome aboard." He turned to a waiter standing by. "Table 305."

Rachel was led away and seated at a round table set for eight people. Another waiter pulled out the chair for her and smiled. Six people were already seated at the table and she felt a little bit like a fish out of water being on her own.

She needn't have worried.

"Hello, I'm David and this is my wife Florence," said a man sitting to her left. He was in his early sixties, Rachel thought, well-dressed, with greying hair, and his wife - who appeared to be some fifteen years younger than him, was glamorous.

"I'm Rachel," she responded and smiled at them both.

"We were just getting to know each other," said a lady opposite. She had bleached blonde hair and was around forty. "This is my husband Greg and I am Sue."

Rachel detected a Scottish accent. She nodded to Greg, who almost disappeared under the table, being quite short.

"I'm Jean and this is Brenda," said the lady next to the empty chair on Rachel's right. The two ladies were probably in their early fifties, and Rachel thought Brenda looked pale.

Animated conversation permeated the restaurant as people settled down for dinner. The place next to Rachel had been set, so the waiters were obviously going to give the eighth diner at table 305 a little more time to arrive before taking their orders.

"Is your partner running late?" asked Greg. A casually dressed man with a moustache, he seemed ill at ease. Rachel thought he must be mid-thirties.

"Sorry?" Then Rachel realised that he was referring to the empty seat. "Oh no. Erm, I'm travelling alone," she managed to say just as a man was seated next to her.

*Blast, it's the man from the deck party.*

"Sorry I'm late," he apologised. "My luggage took longer than expected." His accent was slightly foreign, but Rachel couldn't work out whether it was Italian or Spanish. "I am Carlos."

Carlos gave the impression of someone who was comfortable in his own skin. Rachel wished she could be like that. He managed to charm everyone into easy conversation, including her.

The waiter appeared.

"Good evening, ladies and gentlemen. Welcome to the *Coral Queen*. I am Stavros and this is Geraldine." A young waitress appeared at his side, smiling. "We will be waiting for you over the next few weeks and will do our best to satisfy your tastes."

*Good English, but not perfect*, Rachel noticed. They were given *à la carte* menus with a choice of up to five courses. Rachel's eyes nearly popped out.

The wine waiter, a Bulgarian man called Grigor, had already been to the table and introduced himself. The drinks were arriving during Stavros's introduction.

"Please to enjoy your drinks and we will be back momenta."

Stavros then moved on to the next table.

Rachel noticed Marjorie being seated at a table for two nearby.

"Are you sure you wouldn't like to sit with company?" she overheard Stavros ask.

"No, thank you, I shall be quite happy to eat alone." Marjorie looked overwhelmed and Rachel managed to catch her eye. She smiled, and Marjorie raised her glass of water in salutation.

As soon as Rachel saw Marjorie, she wished she had been seated next to her rather than the overly charming man to her right. She didn't want to be sucked in by anyone's charming ways and was annoyed that a single man had been seated next to her.

*What are they up to? Are they matchmaking?* She realised she was being silly. The Maître D' wouldn't know who she, or Carlos, was.

*It was just a cruel twist of fate.*

Carlos, on the other hand, seemed quite delighted that he had been seated next to her and made every effort to charm her. She decided to be polite, but aloof, and intentionally conversed more with the couple to her left rather than with him.

The dinner passed agreeably. Rachel liked David and Florence. Florence was a paediatrician, and she and David had met when his son had had an accident and had ended up being cared for by Florence. Recently widowed at the time, David had been desperately worried that he would lose his son, too. After the boy had been discharged from hospital, David had sent flowers to Florence and attached his phone number, but Florence had been aware of the ethics of having a relationship with a relative of a patient and had not called him.

"I could stand it no more," David said. "I know it might seem like stalking, but I had to know if she would consider going out with me and so I waited outside the hospital and followed her until she was off-site."

"I was thrilled to see him." Florence continued the story. "I had regretted throwing away his number so that I wouldn't be tempted to call him, and there he stood, in my local café. Of course, I didn't know then that he had followed me or I might have called the police." She nudged him gently at this point.

Rachel was delighted that after a rough time, David had found happiness with this charming woman.

"We waited for twelve months before announcing that we were going out together, which gave me enough time to explain to my son and daughter that I had met someone else. My son didn't mind at all as he already knew Florence, but my daughter, who was fourteen, made things difficult and left home at the earliest opportunity."

"That's the only sad bit," said Florence. "I tried everything to become friends with her, explaining that I didn't want to replace her mother, but she was anger personified. To this day, she hardly acknowledges me, even though she's now twenty-one."

Rachel couldn't imagine anyone disliking Florence, but then, she had not lost her mother at such a tender age so she couldn't judge.

There was only one tricky moment during dinner when conversation lulled and Jean had asked Rachel what she did. The table seemed to go quiet.

"I have just finished a training course and now I work in the public sector." This seemed to satisfy the other guests for now and no-one had asked for further details. Only Florence appeared to want to ask more, but Rachel sensed she understood her not wanting to elaborate.

With dinner over, coffees were served. Rachel had declined wine because she wanted to go to a show and thought she would have a drink in the theatre.

Carlos was hanging back after dinner, and he asked Rachel what she was doing next.

"I'm meeting a friend," she said, even though Sarah had said it would be late before she could join Rachel as she was having to show two new members of the medical team the ropes. Rachel excused herself, saying she had to dash.

In the ladies' room, Rachel came across Marjorie re-touching her lipstick.

"Hello," she said. "Did you enjoy dinner?"

"Yes."

Rachel thought she looked troubled.

"Are you going to the show?" she asked.

"Well, I was going back to my stateroom, but perhaps I will go to the show. I always find it difficult to sleep on the first night of a cruise."

"Perhaps we can go together?" Something about this woman made Rachel want to look after her, and she trusted her instincts.

"That would be nice," replied Marjorie. "Yes please."

Rachel took the old lady's arm, and they walked along from the stern to the bow where the theatre was situated. Rachel noticed Carlos in a crowd of people who were hanging around outside the rest room, and he looked none too pleased when she emerged with Marjorie. He turned his back and walked away.

*Good riddance.*

When she and Marjorie were walking back to their staterooms, Rachel had a feeling they were being watched. The feeling disturbed her, but she forgot all about it when she saw Sarah outside her room.

Sarah was in a different officers' uniform from the one she'd been wearing earlier. "About time too!" She laughed. "Living it up already?"

"For your information, we have just enjoyed a very pleasant show," answered Rachel. "This is my friend, Sarah. Sarah, this is Marjorie."

"Good evening, Lady Snellthorpe," replied Sarah. "The ship's chief medical officer, Dr Graham Bentley, knew your husband, I believe, and he asked me to send his regards and an invitation to join him for dinner tomorrow in the officers' dining room."

"Young Graham, of course! Please tell him I would be delighted," replied Marjorie. "Goodnight to you both, enjoy the rest of your evening. This old lady needs to go to her bed."

Rachel was curious, but not surprised by the conversation. She could tell a woman of breeding when she saw one.

"Goodnight, Marjorie."

Marjorie entered her stateroom feeling happy after spending a pleasurable few hours with the young woman called Rachel. She was delighted that Graham Bentley had remembered her and invited her to join him for dinner the next evening.

She reflected on the evening. The waiter at dinner had asked if she wanted to join other people or sit alone, and she had chosen the latter. In the past, she would have chosen to be sociable, but these days she felt a little edgy in new company and often experienced a need to withdraw herself. The whole cruise idea had become a bit overwhelming without Ralph by her side and she was now wishing she had brought a friend along for company. Johnson had offered to accompany her as had her maid, but she had been convinced she needed to do this by herself.

*Blasted be your stubbornness, Snellthorpe*, Marjorie chided herself. *Oh well, it's too late now, and I will make the best of it.*

On the whole, she viewed the cruise positively. It provided her with an opportunity to strive for independence and show Jeremy that weakness didn't mean walkover.

She had been enjoying people watching over dinner, and when she had seen Rachel seated at the large table, she'd almost asked the waiter to move her. Then she'd scolded herself. *A young woman doesn't want to have an old lady following her around.*

Something else was now troubling Marjorie. *That young man at the table, I'm sure I've seen him somewhere before. Where was it? Oh, how I wish Ralph was here. My mind seems to be meandering these days.*

# Chapter 9

Rachel and Sarah nattered into the small hours.

"I've left my colleague, Bernard, showing the new team members round the ship," Sarah had explained when they'd met at Rachel's door. "And he's agreed to be on call. I have a great team to work with, but it's all change now as we've got a new senior nurse and a new baby doc."

"I'm sure it will be okay, I don't know anyone you can't get along with."

"It's so good to see you, Rachel, but you look like you've lost weight?"

"Only a few pounds, and I'm sure the ship's food will fatten me up. We had a three-course dinner tonight. It could have been five, but I abstained from two. I'm not used to that amount of food as you well know."

"I know. The food is wonderful, but you can't eat like that for too long. We get to eat in the officers' dining room, and sometimes at the infamous midnight buffet. A lot of staff aren't allowed in guest areas of the ship and rarely get above water level."

"That must be awful," sympathised Rachel. "It is rather upmarket, isn't it?"

"Yes. It's great fun as a nurse, although extremely tiring. Many of the crew work twelve to fourteen hours a day, and then they drink too much and romp too much in their time off."

"Really? Like being back at uni, then?"

"Worse because some of them don't have a clue about the meaning of safe sex and when they're drunk, they will go with anyone. We have a few who are renowned Casanovas and are always needing treatment for VD."

"Yuck, that doesn't sound so good. Don't tell me more or I won't be able to look the stateroom stewards in the eye."

"They're not all bad. Many of the Philippinos are married with families back home. They work to send money home so that their families can have a better life. Fidelity is not unheard of, but the bad are bad. Who is your steward?"

"Her name is Josie and I think she is from the Philippines."

"Yes, she is, and very hard working. You will be well catered for."

Rachel enjoyed hearing Sarah's stories while they shared a bottle of red wine, until eventually Sarah fell asleep. Rachel had pulled out the sofa bed in the room for Sarah so that they could chat until they were tired.

It took Rachel a little while to get used to the night time ship noises. She could hear the constant humming of air conditioning and engine noise, along with the rocking of the ship as it negotiated its way through waves. Eventually the rocking became soothing and lulled her into a slumber. She saw Carlos's face just before falling into a deep sleep.

By the time Rachel woke up, Sarah had left for work. She'd explained that she would need to return to her cabin to change her uniform before going to morning surgery. Rachel's room was really dark, but once she opened the heavy curtains, light flooded in. She could only see the sea as she was on the right-hand side of the ship, facing the Atlantic as the ship headed south. The sky was relatively clear, and it looked like it might be a sunny day.

Rachel decided to go and explore the gym, maybe go for a run before breakfast, so she pulled on a tracksuit and made her way to the upper decks. The gym was on deck sixteen, and she was pleased to see that there were only a few people using the facility. A small Indian woman sat behind the desk and smiled at Rachel as she entered.

"Welcome, madam." She spoke perfect English. "Are you familiar with gym equipment?"

"Yes, I am."

"Okay, madam, help yourself. The female changing rooms are over there." She pointed to her left and then she handed Rachel a fresh white bath towel.

Rachel spent forty-five minutes working out on the treadmill, the bike and the rower, and felt a lot better for it. She then decided to go for a shower and postpone her run until the next day. All the while, Carlos's face kept popping into her mind. She became annoyed with herself for thinking about him although she was willing to admit to herself that he was attractive. Drop dead gorgeous, actually, but she didn't want to fall for his obvious charm, nor have a holiday romance that would go nowhere. Another part of her, though, was warming to the idea of a fling which showed that her heart was mending. It must be if she could be attracted to another man after what had seemed like a lifetime of pain. *You're getting ahead of yourself. All he has done is be polite over dinner.*

On the way back to her room, she saw Marjorie waiting for a lift. The old lady smiled.

"Good morning, my dear. It looks like you have been active already this morning."

"Good morning, Marjorie. Yes, I went to the gym, and now I'm just going to change for breakfast. Where are you heading?"

"I'm going to the main restaurant. What about you?"

"I think I'll head up to the buffet for breakfast – I saw it on my way down, then I'll take a tour of the ship."

"You have a good day, dear."

"Oh, I nearly forgot! Sarah invited me to dine in the officers' dining room tonight and she said she would pick us both up at around six. Is that alright with you?"

"That would be perfect. I'll see you then."

Rachel thought that Marjorie seemed a little more relaxed and wondered if she had been imagining the worry in her face. Sarah had explained that the chief medical officer had known Marjorie's husband well and that she and he had been very close, so understandably she must be missing him. *It's a shame she has to travel alone.*

Rachel got lost at least three times while she was strolling around the ship. She found it hard to familiarise herself with the huge floating five-star hotel, which seemed to offer every amenity going. The theatre she had attended the previous night at the front of the ship ran over two decks, providing a balcony and a stalls area. She found a cinema on deck fourteen, but noticed there was not a deck thirteen.

Her father had told her that sailors were very superstitious.

"If Apollo 13 had been a ship, it would never have been called that, and," he'd argued, irrationally, "it would never have got stuck in space."

"Really, Dad, the name caused the problem?" Rachel had given him her most derisive look.

"Mock me if you will, but sailors would never risk it."

"You're supposed to be a man of faith. How can you believe in such nonsense?"

"It's because I am a man of faith that I know there is more to the world than what we see."

Rachel had given up, exasperated.

Continuing her tour of the ship, she found a nightclub next to the cinema for those who wanted to stay up late. Bars were scattered throughout the ship and they all had different names that she didn't try to remember. The jogging area went the whole way around the ship on deck sixteen. On the upper decks, she discovered some false grass and a barbecue area, and there was a golf simulator somewhere, but she couldn't remember where she had seen it.

When she tired of trying to remember where everything was, she paused for a while and looked down from an inner rail to the pools where the party had been the night before. The grill bar was well and truly open and people were already lying on sunbeds with waiters walking around, serving drinks. Rachel saw that there were large racks containing blue-striped towels that could be used for the loungers and for drying after a swim. It had turned into a pleasant though not a hot day, but that did not deter people from wearing the flimsiest of bikinis and trunks.

Rachel also noted that there was a large outdoor cinema screen on the deck where she stood. In her room the previous night, she had found a *Coral News* magazine that listed all of the day's activities. She decided to go and get it from her room and find a quiet place to read.

She turned to leave.

"Rachel. What a nice surprise!"

Rachel felt slightly unnerved. "Carlos, hi. Have you been touring the ship?" she spluttered her words out.

"I have been wandering around for hours admiring the beauty of the ship, and now I see so much more beauty before my eyes."

She felt herself redden. Why did this man have such an effect on her? She decided to ignore the remark and was about to reply when she saw a furrow in his brow as he glanced away from her. Following his gaze, she studied the people below them but couldn't work out who, or what, had attracted his attention. She did spot Marjorie, though, making her way along the deck below.

Carlos quickly looked away, and Rachel surmised that he must just have been looking around.

"There is indeed much beauty to be seen on this ship."

He laughed as he looked towards the women bathing in the pool.

"Well, enjoy your day."

Annoyed and bemused, Rachel moved away.

*Was I mistaken? If not, what had drawn his attention to the lower deck? There are so many people walking around, he must have noticed some bombshell to set his sights on.* Rachel did not kid herself that she would be this man's only interest.

Rachel spent the rest of the day enjoyably reading a tense spy thriller, and the hours passed quickly. Against her better judgement, she had lunch at the grill bar and consumed more fat in that one meal than she normally ate in a week. After a whole day without thinking about Robert, which in itself was progress, she felt the tension of the past few months leaving, and admitted to herself that Sarah had been right to cajole her into taking this break.

The mysterious Carlos did keep cropping up in her thoughts though.

*It's perhaps as well I'm eating elsewhere tonight.*

Rachel dressed for dinner in a smart deep-blue cocktail dress which complemented her figure and clung to all the right curves. It was low cut, but not revealing. Her long blonde hair was brushed through and she had used curling tongs to add some waves. She applied her makeup in a simple way that highlighted her face. Looking in the mirror, she could see that she already had a healthy glow. Her eyes looked an even deeper blue than usual thanks to the reflection of the dress, and she looked happy.

Sarah was smug. "You look beautiful," she said. "But then you would look beautiful in a carrier bag! You are glowing."

"Thank you, and you look rather gorgeous yourself in that uniform. You know about men and their uniform fantasies."

They giggled. Their friendship had picked up where it had left off as all good friendships do.

Marjorie was ready and waiting for them when they knocked at her door.

"Hello, Lady Snellthorpe," said Sarah.

"Oh, do call me Marjorie." The old lady smiled.

"You look lovely," said Rachel, admiring Marjorie's dress sense. She had donned a Ralph Lauren evening dress of pale green and a chiffon scarf to match. Her shoes and handbag were a darker green, and they complemented her clothes. The ship was warm, but she wore a light jacket.

"And you look gorgeous," Marjorie said to Rachel.

"What did you do with yourself today?" asked Rachel.

"I spent most of the day in the ship's library, apart from one venture outside on the lido deck to get some fresh air. The day passed by nicely, and I read a travel adventure about a couple who trekked through Nepal, which provided some light entertainment." She winked at them. "It made me want to be twenty again."

Marjorie still looked spritely for her age – Sarah had told Rachel she would be eighty-five this year.

"You are looking well," Rachel said.

"Yes, I'm thankful that apart from a bit of high blood-pressure, I am in good health. I occasionally use a stick for support as my hips are not as strong as they used to be, but I can walk for miles on the flat. I may decide to go out on deck later. One of the things Ralph and I loved to do was to look at the stars at night."

Sarah linked arms with Marjorie and they started the long walk along the corridor to the lifts. As soon as they arrived in the officers' dining room, a dapper man in his late fifties came towards them. Rachel noticed he was in uniform with three gold stripes on his epaulettes. He was around six feet tall with a muscular physique, and the only sign of the good life was a slight belly paunch. His engaging smile reached his dark brown eyes, and his short fair hair only had a hint of grey to the sideburns.

"Lady Snellthorpe, how wonderful it is to see you again." He took her hand and lightly kissed it. Rachel felt she had been transported into a 1950s movie, but she warmed to his chivalry. "And you must be Rachel?"

"This is Rachel, my best friend, and this is Dr Graham Bentley, our chief medical officer," Sarah said, laughing.

"How do you do, Doctor."

"Tonight, you can call me Graham."

"Only if you call me Marjorie," interjected Marjorie.

"Come along then, Marjorie," he said and put her arm through his before leading them towards a table set for six.

"I hope you don't mind, but Lord and Lady Fanston will be joining us. I believe you know them, Marjorie."

Rachel noticed a slight reticence on Marjorie's part.

"A little. They are friends of my son Jeremy, really. I met them at a fundraising event that Ralph organised. They came along with Jeremy and his then wife, Flora."

"I didn't realise," said Graham, looking a bit embarrassed at inviting the couple. He didn't let it show for long though. Years of medical training had obviously given him the ability to hide his feelings. "They said they were friends, so I invited them along, hoping that they would look after Lady Snellthorpe during the cruise," Rachel heard him whisper to Sarah. Rachel saw for a brief moment that he was obviously annoyed.

As it turned out, a note was delivered to the table to say that Lady Fanston was suffering from seasickness and could Dr Bentley look in on her later? The evening passed in a pleasant, convivial manner and Rachel warmed to the charming but professional CMO. He made a fuss of Marjorie, who had visibly brightened when she heard the Fanstons wouldn't be joining them.

"I don't think she likes them," whispered Sarah to Rachel.

"No, I don't think so either. She is such a nice lady; it's so sad when people lose their soulmates, isn't it?"

"We're not going there tonight. Come on, get some champagne down you. To brighter days ahead."

Sarah clinked her glass against Rachel's in a toast.

"To brighter days ahead."

# Chapter 10

Rachel walked Marjorie back to her room after the meal. Sarah was on-call and had been called away to an emergency after the main course. Apparently, a lady had fallen from a bar stool in one of the bars and the baby doc was already dealing with a crew member who was showing signs of appendicitis.

"It's interesting, getting the inside scoop into what goes on during a cruise," Marjorie said. "I had never given it much thought before, but I suppose, with thousands of passengers and crew on board, accidents and illnesses do occur."

"Yes, Sarah told me there is never a dull moment in the life of a ship's nurse. It's certainly not a revolving holiday for her, but she loves the work, and she does get to see parts of the world that she would never have seen otherwise. She has already been around the world once – not everyone can say that at twenty-five."

"Or eighty-five, dear. Ralph loved cruises in later life, but when we were younger, travel wasn't quite so easy and business kept him tied to England for most of his life. I'm pleased we got to travel over the past twenty years, and we had some marvellous holidays. There were some countries Ralph would never visit though. I would have loved to visit Asia and Africa but Ralph was never that adventurous. He loved Europe, and we often travelled to the USA, so I can't complain."

"You must miss him," Rachel replied with genuine compassion.

Marjorie sighed. "I do, but we had a wonderful marriage and not everyone can say that. You mustn't feel you have to look after me, you know. I am quite alright, and you are a young woman who needs to enjoy your cruise and spend time with young people, not an old codger like me."

"Oh, I am enjoying it so far, and you should understand that you are a delight to be with. I think you're as sharp as any of my friends. I like your company and I don't think you need looking after."

They said goodnight and Marjorie entered her stateroom. She had enjoyed another pleasant evening, apart from the near miss with the Fanston's. Marjorie hadn't elaborated over dinner, but she had not taken to the couple when she'd met them. They had spent the whole evening telling everyone how much they did for charity, but they didn't contribute to the fundraising at all. Ralph had been furious with Jeremy as they hadn't even paid for their tickets. Jeremy had given them tickets and seemed to want to impress them. The whole idea of the ticket price was that it paid for the dinner adding a little bit to the charity for those who didn't donate on the night. There had been a row between father and son, and Ralph had looked quite ill at the end of it.

*Thank goodness for seasickness*, she mused as she got ready for bed.

After walking Marjorie to her room, Rachel decided to go for a walk on the upper decks where she could get some fresh air. The champagne had made her head feel light for a while, but that was wearing off.

As she opened a door to go outside, a huge draught of air almost knocked her over and she noticed the ship lurching up and down a lot more than it had done during the day, even though she was in the midships area. They were travelling through the Bay of Biscay, and the captain had said in his announcement this evening that the sea would be slightly choppy overnight.

"Take that as captain-speak for nasty storm," Sarah had warned. "That means I am in for a very busy night – the Bay of Biscay can be a nightmare when it's rough, but don't worry, this baby is one of the best in the fleet and she will cope with the journey without too much discomfort. The stabilisers prevent her from rocking too much."

Rachel wasn't afraid of the sea. She liked the idea of seeing huge, undulating waves crashing against the ship, knowing that the liner could take it.

She didn't think she would be staying out on deck for long as the wind was picking up. Even on a ship this size, she was struggling to keep her feet on the ground. She noticed members of the crew tying things down to stop them from disappearing over the side. The man-overboard scenario at the emergency drill the previous night had made some passengers laugh at the time, but it was not funny to contemplate someone going overboard in seas like this, and she shuddered at the thought.

Passengers were now being encouraged to move inside, so Rachel went back in to the safety and the warmth of the internal areas. Once inside, she went and sat in one of the lounges where jazz music was playing. She liked jazz, but after rebuffing the interests of a few men who had been drinking heavily, she decided to retire to her room.

*Why can't they just leave me alone?*

She was still feeling like she was being watched, and no matter how much she told herself that she was being paranoid, she found the feeling difficult to shake off.

When she got back to her stateroom, she became more rational. She was not used to men approaching her all the time, but then, she had never been on a cruise by herself.

*That must be what's unsettling me.*

She stood out on the balcony for a while, watching the swell of gigantic waves. Huge breakers crashed into the side spraying the hull, but they were way below where she was standing. Because her room was in the bow of the ship, it was tossed up and down more than those in the middle.

The activities on *Coral Queen* produced a lot of light pollution, even in the vast darkness of the ocean. There were no other ships visible, and she couldn't see any stars through the overcast sky. Rachel could just about make out the moon in the distance. The cacophony of sound produced by the waves rose above the noise of the musical activities on the lower decks.

Finally, at around 2am. Rachel went inside and climbed into bed.

An hour later, an unfamiliar noise woke her. The ship was still rocking up and down and side to side, but it now sounded like someone was trying to get into her room.

*Maybe it's Sarah.*

Bleary eyed and unsteady on her feet, she made her way to the door. Looking through the spy hole out into the corridor, she could only see the wall opposite. She unlocked the double lock and opened the door cautiously. Her heart raced as apprehension gripped her and she put her head outside to see where the noise was coming from. The corridor was clear.

At that moment, someone tapped her from behind. She almost leapt out of her skin, but managed to suppress a scream.

An American voice she recognised from the room next to hers broke the silence.

"Are you alright?"

"Yes, I thought I heard a noise, but it must have been the storm."

"Did it sound like someone trying to get in your room, ma'am?"

"Yes, it did."

"Don't worry, it was a drunk trying to get into the room next door to you. I saw him off. He was on the wrong deck."

"Oh, I see," said Rachel, suddenly becoming aware that she was wearing a flimsy cotton nightdress and was in the corridor in the middle of the night with a man. "Thank you, I think I'll go back to bed now." Then she turned to him again. "What did the man look like?"

"Let me see now – just over six foot, but he wore a hat and scarpered pretty quickly when he realised he was in the wrong corridor. It happens a lot on cruise ships, ma'am, don't be alarmed. The old lady didn't come out so I guess she didn't hear."

The man turned and went back to his room, and Rachel closed her door, but she couldn't get back to sleep. The ship was still being tossed about, but this wasn't what was keeping her awake. Was it a coincidence that someone was trying to get into Marjorie's room, or was there something sinister going on? Carlos's face came back into her head – had he been watching Marjorie when she had met him on the deck the previous day? What was going on?

She told herself that she needed to get some perspective. Her police training and experiences were starting to give her a warped view of the world. Sarah had said it was the same for nurses: they see so much illness that it is sometimes hard to believe that there are people in the world who are healthy.

*Could that be what is happening to me?* Rachel had spent so much time catching criminals that maybe she thought a criminal lurked around every corner. She pulled a pillow on top of her head. *Oh boy, I need this holiday.*

# Chapter 11

After a very restless and disturbed night, Rachel awoke to a knock on the door. She staggered to answer in the dark and was greeted by the ever-cheerful Josie.

"Sorry, madam... Rachel, I was going to do your room. I didn't realise you were asleep. Shall I come back later?"

"Yes, please."

As Rachel closed the door, the first thing she noticed was that the ship was moving normally with just a slight rocking motion. She opened the curtains to a glorious, clear sky, and she couldn't believe it when she looked at her watch and realised it was 11am.

She picked up the phone and asked for coffee to be sent to her room and then went for a shower. When she got out of the shower, she heard a knock at the door and a kitchen waitress brought in a pot of coffee. Rachel gave her a tip and closed the door behind her. She had left the demons of the previous night in her bed and told herself to relax and enjoy her holiday.

Opening the doors on to the balcony, she sat outside with her coffee. It was warm, and although the sun was more or less above the ship, she could see the reflection shining on what was now a calm blue sea. It was as if last night had never happened and the morning had cleaned everything away – the angry sea had gone; the threatening dark and the tumultuous thoughts had all disappeared with it. She was on a cruise ship with a lovely old lady in the room next door and her friend close by. There was absolutely nothing disturbing going on, except in her head.

The phone in her room rang.

"Hello."

"Hi, Rachel. How was your night?" It was Sarah.

"Alright. considering the storm," Rachel replied, deciding to forget about the weird events. "Were you busy?"

"Afraid so. Anyway, I am calling to see if you want to meet up this afternoon for an hour. I am busy the rest of the day."

"Yes, that would be great." They arranged to meet later and Sarah hung up.

Having looked through the *Coral News* at the activities for the day, Rachel decided to have lunch and then go to an art auction. Not that she could afford to buy any art, but she liked looking at paintings by famous artists, and she enjoyed window shopping. In addition to that, there was the offer of free champagne. After the auction, she would meet Sarah for tea, and then take it from there. She had planned to discuss her concerns about the visitor in the night with Sarah. However, this morning she was able to shrug them off and decided that her friend had enough to think about without worrying that Rachel was losing her mind.

During the night, Rachel had decided to ask Marjorie if anything was bothering her, without telling her about the man at her door. She concluded that it would just put unconfirmed suspicions into an elderly lady's head and frighten her unnecessarily. In addition, Marjorie might think the girl she had befriended was a bit unhinged and start avoiding her. The morning light had brought back the rational Rachel, and it was that person who was going to enjoy her cruise.

The weather had turned much warmer as the ship headed south towards Lisbon. The capital of Portugal was to be the first land stop of the trip. Rachel dressed in a pair of smart-casual white cotton trousers and a short-sleeved pink cotton top, then donned a pair of pink sandals.

She went for a buffet lunch and found herself a salad to eat, amazed at how much food people managed to pile onto their plates all in one go. The buffet was noisy and busy, and she wondered whether others had also missed breakfast or whether they ate like this at every meal.

After eating, she made her way to deck fourteen, above the lido deck, and found a single sun lounger free.

This part of the deck formed a circle similar to a balcony, and steps led from it down to the pool. Rachel sat on the sun lounger for a while, observing her surroundings. She could clearly see the swimming pool, spa and children's pool below. The pool was large enough for a swim, but only half the length of the pool she was used to, and far too busy to tempt her in.

A band set up on the stage as the smell of burgers and sausages wafted through the air from her left. The grill bar seemed to be permanently open and especially popular, and she noticed for the first time an ice cream bar next to the cocktail bar to her right.

The pools were at the back of the ship, away from the quieter areas. She watched as people left towels on the sun loungers when they went off for lunch in the buffet bar – something that was strictly forbidden. Other people were walking around, looking for loungers, and Rachel thought it was unfair that most of them had been reserved, but it was not her responsibility so she left it to the pool attendants to prevent this from happening.

Waiters made regular rounds, offering people drinks. Some people were sleeping in the sun, which Rachel knew they would regret later. Some people were applying sun cream frequently and reminding their children to do the same while others were not bothering.

*Poor Sarah – it will be sunburn she will be treating later on.*

Rachel realised she didn't have any sun cream with her so she sat in the partial shade. As she was one of the few people not wearing a bathing costume, she wasn't too worried.

After watching people for a while, she turned to face the sea and got her book out to read as she had half an hour before the art auction started. She heard a familiar voice to her left and was dismayed to see Carlos chatting to a young woman in his normal charming style. She tried not to look, but couldn't help herself.

He looked even more handsome today as the sun's rays were dancing in his hair. He had on a pair of khaki shorts that stopped just above the knees, and she could see his legs were as brown as his arms. His calves were strong and muscular as if he worked out, and he was wearing flip-flops. He was carrying his t-shirt in his left hand, and his torso was just as she'd expected: toned, but not overly worked-out.

Moving her gaze up to his head, she noticed how his jawline was perfectly set in his face. Not a feature was out of place, except, if she was being picky, his ears, which stuck out ever so slightly. He smiled at the woman he was talking to and his white teeth contrasted with his tanned face.

Rachel was just about to see who he was talking to when the woman moved and he caught her looking at him. She looked away quickly as he came towards her.

"There you are," he said. "I have been looking for you everywhere. I was most dismayed not to see you at dinner last night."

"I had dinner with my friend in the officers' dining room." For some reason, she didn't mention the presence of Marjorie. She wanted to ask him who he had been talking to, but thought that would give him too many signals that she was interested.

"I see, my loss was their gain. Did you enjoy hobnobbing with the officers?"

Rachel didn't like the insinuation, and before thinking, replied rather sharply, "I had a lovely dinner with my friend. Not that it's any of your business."

He looked a little bit taken aback, and then, with a pretence at hurt, he said, "I did not mean to offend you, but you must realise that any man who sees you would want to get to know you better."

His smile disarmed her, and she laughed.

"You say some crazy things." She saw he was about to sit on the side of her lounger and she got up quickly. "Would you like this lounger? I'm afraid I need to go."

"Mamma Mia! You can't leave so soon. Where are you going?"

"To the art auction on deck six."

"I was just on my way there myself, so in that case, I shall accompany you." Before she could protest, he had helped her to her feet and was marching her off towards the lifts.

They arrived at the auction in plenty of time and registered their presence. They were each given a bidding card in case they wanted to buy anything and were encouraged to browse the lots, which Rachel was keen to do.

The auction lots were originals and limited edition prints in various sizes and formats, all numbered. The large pieces with elaborate frames were standing on easels, and smaller pieces were hanging on makeshift walls.

Carlos made polite conversation, but he did stand back and allow her to browse, giving the appearance of browsing himself. He looked distracted, glancing around as if he was waiting for someone.

*That girl he was speaking to upstairs, I suspect.*

Then he moved away and left her browsing for a while.

She wasn't going to let his presence spoil her appreciation of all the art pieces and she paused to look at some prints by the Ukrainian artist Anatole Krasnyansky. She liked brightly coloured work, and his held a mixture of surrealism with a sense of structure and purpose. She was looking at a print of his *Russia Red Sunset* when she lost sight of Carlos.

She sighed and moved around the room, looking at the many varied prints. There was even a Picasso original for sale.

Other prints she browsed were by Salvador Dali and Thomas Kinkade. There were hundreds to look at, and after about an hour, she realised that the auction was about to start.

Carlos appeared by her side.

"Shall we find a seat?" he asked and handed her a glass of champagne.

"There are two over there." Rachel pointed out.

"Oh no, these will be better just there." He led her away to two seats that weren't very well positioned at all. As she sat down, she saw Marjorie three rows in front on the opposite side to where they were seated.

Carlos must have realised Rachel was looking at him, perplexed.

"I thought I saw a friend over there from Rome, but it is not him," he said quickly.

His explanation was perfectly plausible, and it was a packed auction room.

*It's just a coincidence.*

The auction began with a rather prolonged introduction and sales pitch, followed by a few giveaways. After this, the paintings were brought to the front one by one and auctioned off.

It was actually quite exciting. Rachel could have afforded some of the cheaper lots, but she didn't want to spend her spare cash at the moment. She noticed Marjorie bidding for a Dali. Rachel was not surprised that Marjorie would like art and having a spend might help ease some of the pain she must be going through. The bidding was in US dollars, and Rachel was trying to do the calculations in her head. Marjorie bought the painting for around £2,500 by her calculation.

After about an hour, Rachel looked at her watch and turned to Carlos.

"I need to go, I'm afraid. I am meeting my friend, Sarah, for tea before she goes into evening surgery."

"Will I see you at dinner?" he whispered.

"I will be there, so yes," she replied.

She waited for him to move, but realised that he was staying so she got up and left. The confused thoughts returned again as she made her way down to deck five where she would meet Sarah. She liked Carlos and was definitely attracted to him, and she sensed he was attracted to her, too, but there was something else going on that she couldn't put her finger on. It was like an itch that couldn't be scratched and it was disturbing.

She saw Sarah as she walked down the stairs into the main atrium, realising that she hadn't been inside any of the shops on board yet. The sea days were flying by. Sarah greeted her warmly, and they moved into the patisserie which was less busy than the other areas because passengers had to pay for cakes and drinks in there.

Sarah smiled at one of the waiters and he came over to serve them.

"I'll have a cappuccino and a slice of that delicious looking strawberry cake," said Sarah.

"A coffee for me and a slice of blackcurrant cheesecake, please," said Rachel, handing over her payment card.

"No payment, ma'am." He smiled at Sarah before walking away.

"Oh, he's sweet on you," said Rachel, laughing.

"He's nice, from the Czech Republic. We met in surgery two weeks ago. He's been following me around ever since, but in a nice rather than a weird way."

"I'm pleased you know the difference," said Rachel, thinking of a few of the stalkers she had had to deal with as a policewoman. No stalking was acceptable, but it was hard to differentiate between the annoying-but-harmless kind and the downright dangerous kind. The police took the problem much more seriously than they had in the past, and Rachel told Sarah how her sergeant was obsessive about it.

"He's probably been burned in the past. I bet someone ended up seriously harmed or even killed," said Sarah. "I have worked with doctors who have become so cautious that they end up wasting thousands of pounds ordering unnecessary tests. It's usually because they missed a cancer and a patient died as a result. Some doctors never forgive themselves while others accept their own fallibility."

"You're right. He let someone go that he should have charged, and they went on to kill. I have arrested some right scumbags, who are relatively harmless, and then I arrest someone who appears to be an outstanding citizen, but there is something in the eyes that makes me want to lock them away for the rest of their lives. Of course, it ends up being down to the courts and how much evidence we can gather. Then there are people who drop charges before it goes to court. It's a complicated world out there. Anyway, tell me more about the waiter. Do you like him?"

"If you mean *like*-like, then no. He's nice enough, but not my type. I'm a bit wary of cruise ship relationships because word gets around and life is just too hectic. I could do without the complications."

"What's your new baby doc like then?" asked Rachel.

"He's nice. His name is Alessandro Romano, but thankfully he prefers Alex. He's good under pressure, which is what we need because he has to do the bulk of the work while Graham goes off seeing passengers who don't really need him, but who demand to be seen. Alex has already had to deal with the broken wrist of an engineer and a miscarriage of a crew member."

"Oh dear, poor woman. I didn't think you could deal with all that sort of stuff on board."

"It's amazing, Rachel, what we can do. We have X-ray machines, scanners, and a blood lab. The only thing we can't do is operate, so sometimes we have to do an evacuation. The woman will need to go to hospital in Lisbon for a check-up. The other thing we have," Sarah whispered, "is a morgue."

Rachel had taken a few trips to morgues and seen a post-mortem as part of her training, but it was not something she wanted to think about.

"By the way," she said instead, "I think you are going to be seeing some lobsters tonight as there were loads of people out by the pool without sun cream."

"I suspected as much. People forget how damaging the sun can be out at sea because they feel a breeze."

They moved on from work talk and Rachel decided to tell Sarah about Carlos.

"I've been a bit silly. I have met this guy called Carlos who sits at my dinner table. I noticed him on the lido deck the first day of the cruise because he's really handsome and he seems interested, but what's the point? It's just a two-week holiday."

"A two-week holiday where you could have some fun. Just take it as it comes and try not to stress about it – if something comes of it, then great. If not, you will have had a nice holiday and some fun with a guy, no strings attached."

"You might be right, you know, but then you could let your hair down a bit and find some handsome officer to go out with."

"Maybe I will. Changing the subject, I have got shore leave tomorrow as Alex and Brigitte are staying on board. I think she's quite sweet on him, but the new senior, Gwen, will be staying behind too, so she won't get a look-in."

"Oh yes. You haven't told me about your new senior."

"Nothing to tell. Workaholic, but okay – you know the type."

After Sarah had left, Rachel changed for dinner and felt excited anticipation about seeing Carlos. She'd decided to take Sarah's advice and just enjoy his company without pinning any hopes on it becoming a romance.

Looking in the mirror, she was pleased with what she saw. She had chosen a maroon cocktail dress that her father had bought her when he took her shopping before the cruise. He had insisted on kitting her out with enough dresses, including evening dresses for the three formal nights when the captain and crew would be present, and champagne and canapés would be served before dinner. This dress was ideal for this evening. It accentuated her figure without being over-dressy – she didn't want to appear to be making too much of an effort. It was a hard balance, but she felt that she had achieved it.

A light smattering of makeup and her hair flowing freely, she put on a shawl to cover her shoulders during dinner: a rule for diners eating in the main restaurant. As she left her room, she was feeling slightly nervous.

*So much for being relaxed about it,* she admonished herself, but smiled happily nonetheless. She hadn't thought about Robert for two whole days, and that had to be good.

David and Florence were pleased to see her.

"We missed you last night," Florence said kindly.

"I have a friend who works on the ship so we met for dinner," answered Rachel.

"You look radiant," said Brenda, who was already seated with Jean.

Rachel blushed, and then as she heard the voice behind her, she blushed even more. Thankfully the lighting was dim and people were chatting so they didn't notice.

"Good evening." Carlos announced himself. "How beautiful the ladies look tonight." His eyes swept the table, but rested on Rachel. "How was tea with your friend?" he enquired.

"It was very nice, thank you. How was the end of the auction?"

"I didn't stay long," he answered. Rachel got the feeling he wasn't being entirely honest.

*Perhaps he's a compulsive liar.*

She smiled at him.

# Chapter 12

On the third morning of the cruise, the ship was docked in Lisbon.

The day before, Marjorie had met another widow, Freda, while playing bridge in the card room on board ship. They'd got chatting and were both pleased to find someone to share time with. Freda, Marjorie had discovered, had been the wife of an ex-diplomat and had been based in various embassies around the world. They had moved back to Scotland when Freda's husband had retired and spent many happy years catching up with old friends and family.

"My husband died a year ago following a stroke," explained Freda. "He was out playing golf when he collapsed, and unfortunately he never regained consciousness. It's perhaps as well," she continued. "He would have hated being disabled and was a firm believer in euthanasia."

Marjorie could empathise with Freda with regard to the sudden loss of a spouse after decades of marriage. "It must have been hard," she said, remembering how hard it still was for her after Ralph's death.

"It was awful, to be honest. I just wanted to die myself. If it hadn't been for the children and grandchildren, I'm not sure what I would have done. I don't even like to think about it. I still find it difficult to go on sometimes, even with the support of family – the days and nights can be so long, can't they?"

"Yes, they can," Marjorie acknowledged. "Life is never the same, that's for sure."

Marjorie realised how cathartic it had been to talk to someone about her loss. *Another person who understands the deep sense of grief which nothing will alleviate.* When Marjorie had discovered Freda was going on the same trip in Lisbon the next day, she had been delighted.

Marjorie had been seated close to Rachel the previous evening and thought she had looked very happy. She still couldn't remember where she had seen the man who was with her before, though, in spite of racking her brains for two days.

*Oh, old brain, I wish you could remember things.*

She had gone to bed, deciding to think about it before she went to sleep. She had read somewhere that if you thought about something before going to bed that you would remember it during the night.

It didn't work.

Marjorie and Freda met up at breakfast, and afterwards went along to the theatre, where groups were gathering to join their various coach trips. Marjorie had booked the trip on the first day and was looking forward to visiting the Gulbenkian Museum, renowned for its private art collection. After that, they would be taken on a narrated tour through Lisbon, and she and Freda had decided they would stop off at the far end of the harbour and visit one of the larger hotels for afternoon tea.

The museum turned out to be everything Marjorie had expected, and more. It was huge and spacious inside as they entered through the main hallway. As they were on a tour, they had round stickers with numbers attached to their chests, and followed the tour guide who explained about the collections, but they only managed to see a fraction of the exhibits due to time constraints.

"You could spend a week in here and still not see everything," Marjorie remarked.

"Yes, I agree. I do love art, don't you? It's a shame we won't have time to see the Lalique collection as well."

Marjorie also liked Lalique and had a few pieces of the glassware herself. René Lalique was famous around the world for his unmistakable style of glass sculptural design. He produced anything from small sculpted animals to large bowls and vases and his work was sought after worldwide. Nevertheless, she was much more interested in paintings, and thrilled to see works by

Rubens, Rembrandt and Turner. There were also pieces by Renoir, and she was in her element admiring the works of these great masters of art. Delighted with her Dali purchase the previous day, she was taking full advantage of the time they had, browsing the masterpieces.

Freda seemed to be enjoying the sculptures, particularly those that reminded her of her times overseas.

"We saw so many great works of art in many different parts of the world," she said.

Marjorie felt that although her own sense of loss was deep, Freda's seemed to eat her apart. *I wonder if any of us are ever happy again after the loss of our soulmate*s. She chastised herself for being maudlin and reminded herself how both she and Ralph had promised each other they would try to go on and enjoy life if the worst should happen to either of them.

After the museum tour, Marjorie and Freda had lunch in the café before rejoining the coach for the rest of the trip, chatting all the way. Because both of them had been to Lisbon many times before, they didn't feel the need to listen too carefully to the tour guide.

The coach driver dropped a number of passengers off at the far end of the harbour.

"You will need to make your own way back to the ship," the tour guide advised as they left the coach, and they agreed to be back at the *Coral Queen* by five.

Marjorie and Freda sat in the Botanical Gardens for a while, enjoying the scented perfume of the tropical flowers that were grown there. At three o'clock, they decided to find a grand hotel with excellent service and enjoy afternoon tea with cakes and scones.

"It has always surprised me how we British still long for the luxuries of home, even when abroad," said Marjorie. "It's no wonder that some foreigners find us annoying. Did you find this when you lived abroad?"

"Yes," replied Freda. "Seamus always insisted on haggis for Burn's Night, even when we were based in Morocco. It had to be shipped over in a diplomatic pouch." She chortled at the memory. Freda had a lovely laugh, and Marjorie was pleased that she appeared to be happier in herself. They had spent much of the day sharing memories, and Marjorie noticed that Freda had difficulty staying in the present.

Marjorie also noticed that although they were of a similar height and build, the other woman did not appear to pay the same attention to her appearance. Her hair was a little dishevelled whereas Marjorie's was immaculately well styled and groomed. Freda's nails looked worn, and her face showed the marks and lines of someone who had smoked for many years, and who probably liked a drink too many. Marjorie had never smoked, but she did like the occasional brandy at bedtime and drank socially. Perhaps as a diplomat's wife, Freda had spent most of her life having to entertain guests and host parties, so this might have taken its toll on the woman.

Looking out of the window, Marjorie realised it was raining. She looked at Freda.

"Do you have a coat, dear?"

"No, I don't seem to have brought one," Freda replied.

"Never mind," said Marjorie. "I have an umbrella and a jacket. Why don't you wear my coat and hat? I'm always prepared for every eventuality."

"Oh, thank you, that is so kind. If I get wet, my rheumatism plays up awfully."

Freda took the coat and put on the hat as they left the hotel to find a taxi to take them back to the ship. They stood at the side of the road, waiting for a gap in the traffic so that they could cross to the other side. A large crowd gathered around them as everyone seemed to be waiting to cross at the same time.

Marjorie looked across the road and saw Rachel and her friend in the distance, heading their way.

*Perhaps we could all share a taxi…*

Her thoughts were shattered as she heard the loud beep of a vehicle horn, and she watched in horror as a lorry jackknifed right in front of her.

There was a huge commotion, and she looked around for Freda. Moments later, she saw her hat in the road. Her coat, along with Freda, was lying underneath the lorry.

Dropping her umbrella, Marjorie froze to the spot while the rain lashed down onto her head.

# Chapter 13

Rachel had slept well, in spite of feeling some disappointment that Carlos hadn't offered her a kiss on the cheek, or even a clichéd compliment, when they had parted the previous night. In fact, their goodbye had been rather awkward. Putting her disappointment aside, Rachel got up early and worked out in the gym before having breakfast. Then she made her way to the main atrium to meet Sarah.

Sarah arrived around fifteen minutes late, looking tired. She had on a pair of cropped cotton trousers and a white printed cotton t-shirt. Her hair was down today, and the long naturally wavy light-brown locks reached the middle of her back. Rachel admired her friend appreciatively. Both women were used to wearing uniforms in their jobs and enduring the constraints this entailed, including tying back hair and wearing little or no jewellery, but they both liked bling when off duty.

"I'm sorry I'm late." Sarah was still breathless from rushing. "We were up most of the night dealing with burns. One woman had serious sunburn, and we had to arrange for her to go to the burns unit today at the local hospital."

"Will she be okay?"

"Yes, it's just precautionary really, and they can provide her with a supply of dressings to cover the worst of them. She was lucky. I think if she had been out in the sun for much longer, she would have been in trouble. Anyway, that's enough about me. Come on, let's hit Lisbon."

The two women walked off the ship arm in arm, chatting and laughing just like old times. Sarah wanted to go into town first to do some shopping and then they planned to walk the opposite way along the main promenade and see some of the sights that Lisbon Harbour had to offer. As they made their way to the shops, Sarah continued her stories of the previous night.

"Alex was called to see a drunken, abusive passenger in one of the bars who had hit his wife. Graham was seeing another passenger at the time who had not eaten enough following his insulin injection and suffered a hypoglycaemic episode."

Rachel knew that hypoglycaemia was when a diabetic's blood-sugar went too low and they needed immediate treatment before they went into a coma. She had been trained to spot the signs, which can mimic drunkenness, so that she could call the paramedics and initiate first aid where necessary.

"The drunk was too hot to handle for Alex, so security locked him up for the night, while Alex stitched his wife's eyebrow in the surgery."

"Domestic abuse doesn't confine itself to land then?" Rachel asked sadly.

"No, it doesn't, although they usually fight in their rooms. Not in one of the main bars."

"What happens next?"

"We asked the wife if she wanted to press charges and she said no, otherwise we could have had him arrested in Lisbon today. He will get a warning from the chief security officer and told that one more strike, and he's off ship. I expect security weren't too gentle with him, either, because he was fighting them, so he will have a few bruises himself today. The jury will be out as to whether this was a one-off, as his wife claims, or his usual behaviour."

They walked towards the town which was a couple of miles away from where the *Coral Queen* was docked. The temperature was a pleasant 28 degrees centigrade with clear blue skies, but Rachel had picked up from the captain's announcement before she'd left the ship that there was a chance of rain in the afternoon. Each morning and evening, the captain made an announcement over the ship's loudspeaker detailing where they were, at what speed they were travelling, and a weather update for the day or night. The cruise director followed on with announcements about activities available through the day or evening.

Rachel and Sarah arrived at the main square and entered the shopping areas through a large archway forming a gateway. The centre was pedestrianised, the streets cobbled and relatively narrow for a city. They enjoyed a pleasant couple of hours shopping and stopped off for lunch at one of the outside cafés.

Rachel found Sarah easy to talk to because she always listened and digested information before giving an opinion. Conversation flowed freely as they sat at a table, relaxed and replete after their lunch, drinking cappuccinos and watching tourists having their photos taken beside a man dressed as a clown. Rachel pondered whether to tell her friend about her concerns regarding Marjorie, but what was there to tell? A few feelings and a drunk trying to get into Marjorie's room were hardly conclusive proof of any sinister goings on.

"Come on," said Sarah after they'd finished their drinks. "I want to show you the prettier parts of Lisbon."

They got up and left the centre via the same archway through which they had entered and walked back towards the ship.

"We need to walk another couple of miles along the main road on the other side of the ship," Sarah explained.

They passed the *Coral Queen* on their journey, joining an avenue with a hospital on the right-hand side.

"That's a Hospital for Tropical Diseases," said Sarah. Rachel, exhilarated at being on land again, was enjoying the exercise, although the heat was becoming more and more humid.

"I think it's going to rain," she remarked, and Sarah agreed.

They continued their walk and took a right fork on to another avenue, which ran parallel to the one they had been walking along. The roads were busy and there was a lot of traffic noise. Rachel needed to raise her voice to be heard, but the views were lovely.

They came off the main road to visit the Botanical Gardens where they sat for a while and enjoyed ice cream until it started to rain. Neither of them had brought coats. Rachel looked at the skies where the clouds were now looking menacing. The rain was getting heavier, so they sheltered for a few minutes inside a café doorway.

"I think it's time to head back to the ship," said Sarah. "We can get a bus on the main road."

As they were walking towards the main road, Rachel caught a glimpse of Marjorie in the distance on the far side of the road. Crowds were building as people were trying to find shelter or make their way back to the ship. Suddenly there was the sound of a horn and she saw a lorry skidding in the road as the driver tried to slam on his brakes. His lorry jackknifed, blocking the boulevard.

Rachel and Sarah heard screams and immediately ran towards the commotion.

"Oh dear!" exclaimed Sarah. "Those are our passengers. I hope everyone is alright."

As they arrived at the scene, Rachel realised just how serious the situation was. An elderly woman was lying in the road, and Rachel knew she was dead before they got any closer.

"I'm the ship's nurse," called Sarah. "Please stand back and allow some room. Has anyone called for the emergency services?"

"I have," said a shocked-looking man in the crowd. Rachel lifted her head to look away from the body, finding herself relieved to see it wasn't Marjorie. She decided to do some crowd control, asking people to step back onto the pavement. As she did so, she thought she caught a glimpse of Carlos running in the opposite direction. It was only a passing glimpse before she became preoccupied with moving people away from the body.

"Please, everybody, stay around for a while as the police will want to ask if anyone saw what happened."

Rachel, now in full PC mode, noticed that Sarah had obviously decided there was nothing she could do for the woman in the road, and a man had covered the body with his coat. Rachel saw her friend helping the lorry driver, who had bashed his head on the windscreen, and admired the way in which her friend dealt with his injuries while calming him down.

"Is there anyone medical here?" shouted Sarah. Rachel could see she was trying to stem the bleeding from the man's head and keep him talking.

The emergency services arrived a few minutes later and took over from Sarah while the police were already taking notes and statements from people in the crowd. Rachel saw Marjorie standing at the side of the road, looking pale and shaken. She went towards the old lady and put her arm around her. Marjorie was soaking wet, and Rachel saw an open umbrella lying on the ground.

"Come on, Marjorie," she said, as she picked up the umbrella and covered both of their heads. "There's a bench over there. Let's sit you down, and then I will find a policeman to take a statement from you so I can get you back to the ship."

Marjorie tried to smile, but Rachel could see she was badly shaken.

Rachel found a policeman and sent him in Marjorie's direction. She then found Sarah speaking to another policeman and calling the ship. It was obvious that Sarah was going to be awhile as the policeman didn't speak much English and Sarah didn't speak Portuguese. They were trying to converse in Spanish.

"I need to get Marjorie back to the ship," she explained to Sarah.

"I didn't realise she was here. Yes, of course. I need to sort out some things here first. We'll meet up later, after dinner."

Rachel moved back towards Marjorie. The policeman shook his head and said he hadn't managed to get much out of her, but she could return to the ship.

"It appears to have been a tragic accident," he said in heavily accented English as he walked away.

Rachel helped Marjorie to her feet, and they crossed the road to flag down a taxi. Rachel held on to Marjorie's hand on the way back in the taxi. The old lady was shivering with cold and muttering words that were not making any sense.

"Please hurry," Rachel called out to the taxi driver. "This lady needs to see a doctor."

The taxi driver looked in the rear-view mirror and although Rachel was unsure whether he understood her words, she was certain he understood the situation and he put his foot down on the gas. Rachel was becoming increasingly worried as Marjorie became more incoherent and was only semi-conscious. She had found a blanket on the back seat of the taxi and wrapped this around the dear old lady, but this was now wet, too. Marjorie needed dry clothes, and she needed them soon.

"Stay with me, Marjorie," Rachel said, holding the old lady close and trying to warm her up with body heat. Rachel then called Sarah on her mobile phone and explained the situation.

"I'll call ahead and have a medical team waiting for your arrival, but they may turn her around to the hospital," Sarah explained.

"They can't do that!" cried Rachel, feeling hysterical. The taxi driver looked at her in the rear-view mirror again, concern in his eyes. "She would be all alone in a foreign country. They have to care for her."

After what seemed an age, the taxi arrived at the cruise terminal and was ushered straight through. Rachel was relieved to see Dr Bentley waiting on the dockside with a stretcher and a silver space blanket to treat hypothermia. There were two others with him. One was Bernard, and the other, Rachel presumed, was Alex. As soon as the taxi stopped, they opened the doors from the outside and went to work immediately. One of the crew members lifted Marjorie out of the car gently, and Dr Bentley wrapped her in the blanket while Bernard discreetly removed the wet clothing. They worked quickly, and all looked concerned.

"Please don't send her away," Rachel pleaded.

"She needs a hospital," said Dr Bentley.

"No," muttered Marjorie, and Rachel could see fear in her eyes. "No hospital," and then she became incoherent again.

Rachel looked at Dr Bentley, silently imploring him to do as Marjorie wished.

"Quick! Get her to the infirmary."

With that, Marjorie was strapped to the stretcher on wheels and moved swiftly away, with Bernard pulling and Alex pushing.

"Go and get dried off yourself," Bernard called back to Rachel. "Then come to the infirmary on deck two." Rachel was about to argue, but then realised that she was also soaking wet and feeling shivery herself. She started to follow the stretcher, but then she heard a call of dismay from behind her.

"Fare, ma'am. Please?" The taxi driver was following her.

"Oh, I'm so sorry. How much?" Before he had time to answer, Rachel shoved a twenty euro note in his hand, turned towards the ship and ran.

# Chapter 14

Rachel had to queue to get through security for what seemed like an age. There were crowds of passengers waiting for the lifts, carrying bags of shopping following their day out, so she decided to take the stairs. She ran up six flights to her deck and walked briskly down the corridor. By the time she got to her room, she was feeling panicky, and very cold.

*Please don't die, Marjorie.* She kept saying the words to herself, over and over again.

Even in her state of panic, she realised that it would be quicker to take a hot shower to warm up before attempting to change into dry clothes. She put the shower on to the highest setting it would allow and stepped inside – removing her clothes once she was in the shower. She was shivering and her teeth were chattering, and in spite of the warm temperatures outside, she felt frozen. She realised this was partly due to the wet and partly the shock of the events that had just taken place.

Rachel spent a lot longer in the shower than she had intended because her legs had turned to jelly as the adrenaline kicked in as well as the after effects of running up the six flights of stairs on top of all the walking she and Sarah had done. She gave in to exhaustion and sat down in the shower for a while until she felt warmer and her muscles stopped trembling.

She managed to slow her breathing, taking deep breaths to bring her mind and body back under control. Her heart, which had been racing frantically, slowed down as she did this, and she gradually began to feel normal again.

It had taken Rachel almost an hour to compose herself. Now that she was in a condition where she could leave the room, she dressed in a pair of jeans and a light summer jumper over a t-shirt. She then headed down to deck two where she found the medical centre and was greeted by a small, brown-haired girl, she assumed was Brigitte.

"Is Lady Snellthorpe here?" Rachel asked, dreading the reply.

"Yes, she is. Are you Rachel?" The French accent was unmistakeable.

"Yes."

"Follow me. She is on the ward and sleeping. Dr Bentley has given her some sedation, and she is being warmed up as her temperature had dropped below thirty-six degrees centigrade, which is not good for anyone, let alone a woman her age. She's lucky she didn't have a heart attack."

"Will she be alright?" asked Rachel.

Brigitte didn't answer.

They walked into the ward and Rachel saw Marjorie lying on a bed, completely wrapped from head to toe in the silver space blanket. There was a heart monitor beside her, and Rachel could see that Marjorie's heart rate was just fifty beats per minute. She had a drip in her arm, and Bernard was sitting with her.

"I'll leave you with her for a while; I need to go get another IV bag," he said.

Rachel took a seat next to the bed and saw that Marjorie was asleep. The elderly lady looked deathly pale behind the oxygen mask that covered her face.

Bernard came back to the ward and smiled at Rachel.

"This one's a tough cookie," he said brightly. "My money is on her pulling through."

Rachel wasn't sure whether he believed this or whether he was trying to cheer her up, but it had the desired effect. She sighed a huge sigh of relief.

While sitting at Marjorie's side, she had a chance to look around the ship's infirmary and was impressed. It looked like a real hospital ward with four beds and all the modern equipment she was used to seeing when she was accompanying victims or criminals to a hospital on land.

She looked at her watch and realised it was six o'clock. They were due to sail.

"Sarah!" she exclaimed. "Where's Sarah?"

"She's aboard." Dr Bentley entered the ward. "She's had to go and get warmed up herself because she was soaking wet, too. That's the last time she gets shore leave." He was joking, but there was a look of concern in his eyes as he came closer. "She should really be in a hospital, you know, but I have called her son back in England and he has consented to us keeping her on board. He asked to be kept informed. The captain has agreed with my decision to abide by both of their wishes."

As if on cue, the ship's engines started up and Rachel felt slight movement as the *Coral Queen* set sail.

"Was her son alright? Is he flying out to join us at the next stop?" Rachel asked.

"I'm afraid not," whispered Dr Bentley. "In fact, he was rather abrupt."

Rachel was horrified. She would have been on the next plane if it had been her mother.

Dr Bentley checked that all was well with Marjorie and then went to help with evening surgery as it was busy in the waiting area outside. Bernard asked if Rachel was happy to stay with Marjorie while he helped with the surgery as Sarah was supposed to be on duty. Rachel agreed – glad to be alone with her thoughts for a while.

*What was it Marjorie was mumbling about in the taxi? "My fault – my coat." None of it made sense. And did I really see Carlos? If so, why had he been running away rather than helping?*

All of the sinister thoughts of the past three days jumbled themselves around in Rachel's tired mind.

A crew member entered the ward. "Senior asked me to bring you some food, ma'am," he said and laid a tray down on a table which he pulled towards her.

"I'm not sure I can eat anything."

"I'll leave it there, ma'am, just in case. Can I get you anything to drink?"

"A strong coffee, please." She smiled at him. A six-foot-tall Indian man, he had a solid build and was wearing black trousers with a white tunic over the top. His name badge said Raggie. "Is that your name?"

"No, ma'am, but no-one can pronounce my real name, so I decided on Raggie. People still call me Reggie rather than Raggie, though, so I can't win! I am the medical team steward and I make sure they are all looked after good."

Rachel looked at the food as Raggie left the ward. It was fresh salmon and spring vegetables with sautéed potatoes. In spite of saying she didn't feel hungry, she actually managed to eat almost all of it.

*Stress reaction*, she thought as she drank the contents of a whole thermos of coffee.

Every now and again, Bernard or Brigitte popped in to check on Marjorie and write down observations on her chart. Rachel was pleased to see that there was a slight pinkness returning to her face, and her temperature on the monitor was now thirty-six degrees while her heart rate had come up to sixty. Rachel laid her head on the bed, and with flashbacks of lorries, a dead body and crowds of people whirring round in her head, she fell asleep.

"Wake up, sleepy head."

Rachel opened her eyes. "Sarah! Thank goodness you're alright. I thought you'd missed the sailing, but Dr Bentley told me you hadn't."

"It was touch and go for a while because the ship can't wait too long for anyone. I made it in ten minutes before sailing. How are you?"

"What time is it?" asked Rachel, realising that there were no windows in the infirmary.

"Eleven o'clock. I decided to let you sleep."

Rachel looked at Marjorie. The oxygen mask had been removed, and she was still asleep, but her colour was back to normal.

"She'll pull through," Sarah said. "She's going to sleep all night, though, after the sedation, so you should go to bed. Brigitte is going to take care of her for the night."

"What happened to that poor woman?"

"No-one knows. Nobody seems to have seen anything. One minute she was standing waiting to cross the road, and the next minute she was in front of the lorry. The driver had no way of stopping in time in that rain."

"Is he okay?"

"Yes, he went to hospital for stitches and was in shock, but no serious injuries. The lady who was killed had been with Marjorie, according to one couple who were standing close by. The police have settled for tragic accident as far as I'm aware although it could have been suicide."

"Or..." Rachel finally let out what had been nagging her all day. "She could have been pushed."

Sarah looked shocked at the thought, "You're tired, Rachel. Passengers don't get pushed in front of lorries. By all accounts, she was travelling alone, was widowed and had a very close family."

"Is she in your morgue?"

"No, if passengers die ashore, then it is down to the local police to investigate and the coroner will decide on the cause of death. The family have been informed and are flying out to Lisbon. They will be able to repatriate the body once they have identified her."

"I thought Marjorie was going to die in the taxi." Rachel's bottom lip quivered. "She was losing consciousness before my eyes and I was completely helpless. It was horrible." The tears that had been close to the surface came out now that the horror of the day was gone.

"You did the right thing, Rachel. Graham said you saved her life by wrapping her up and using body warmth. He was impressed, and he also said that he wouldn't want to argue with you. What was that all about?"

"I wouldn't know!" Rachel managed a laugh as she remembered how she would have pushed the trolley on board ship herself, or at least been arrested trying, if he hadn't agreed to care for Marjorie.

"Come on, Rachel, it's time for bed. I for one am dead beat."

Rachel kissed Marjorie's forehead, and then Sarah took her arm and led her away. They parted at the lifts and agreed to meet up the next morning as Rachel would be down to check on Marjorie.

"Some holiday you're having so far!" Sarah looked uncertain. "I'm almost feeling guilty for persuading you to take this cruise, and I can assure you that nothing like this happened until you came on board."

Rachel returned to the comfort of her room, feeling stiff from falling asleep in an awkward position, and opened the balcony doors to listen to the sea. She loved the sound of the waves crashing against the ship. She looked up into the sky and could see that it was clear again and the night was warm.

As she lay on her bed, she started to rationalise the events of the day. Tragic accidents did happen, and the old lady could have just tripped into the road. Or maybe she had wanted to end it all and kill herself. It wouldn't be the first time Rachel had come across a widow who couldn't go on after the death of a partner.

*Or she could have been pushed.* The thought popped into her head as she drifted off.

# Chapter 15

Rachel woke at six in the morning and decided to go for a run then to the gym. She pulled on her light cotton sports trousers and a t-shirt and headed up to deck sixteen. The ship was relatively quiet with just a few people milling around. Crew were already hard at work washing down decks and putting out fresh towels. Today was a sea day, and the ship was due to arrive in Barcelona the next day.

Rachel ran around the whole of deck sixteen three times, feeling the need to clear her head. She had put the thoughts of the awful accident in perspective, but she remained concerned for Marjorie. The old lady had looked so frail the day before.

"Good morning." She was dragged back to reality by the presence of another jogger at her side. He was a tall, thin man dressed in shorts and jogging vest with dreadlocks tied in a ponytail.

"Good morning." Rachel smiled back.

"It's a great morning for a run," he continued in his lovely Jamaican accent. "I like to get out before it gets too hot, and as you can see, I don't need a suntan."

Rachel laughed politely, but remained distracted. Any other time, she would have been happy to chat with this lively man, but she stopped running when they got near the gym.

"Enjoy your run," she said.

"Have a great day," he replied and continued jogging.

After a forty-five minute workout, Rachel headed back to her cabin where she showered and changed into a sleeveless cotton sundress before going to deck fourteen for a buffet breakfast. By this time, people were already claiming sun loungers with towels and books before going for breakfast themselves. Children were swimming and calling out gaily to one another. The reflection from the sun created dancing shimmers of light on the sea below, and the clear blue sky promised a beautiful day ahead – very different from the day before.

Rachel was wondering how hot it was going to be today when, as if on cue, the captain's voice came through over the loudspeaker. The sea would be calm and the temperature likely to reach 32 degrees this afternoon. There was a reminder about sun cream, then some other announcements that Rachel couldn't hear over the noise of conversations and the clattering of dishes in the main buffet area.

Rachel helped herself to fruit and muesli and found a table by a window. She could hear a Jamaican man singing as he brought around teas and coffees and recognised him as the happy jogger she had met earlier.

"Coffee, tea?" he would ask in between lines of a song she didn't recognise.

"We meet again, beautiful lady," he said as he poured her a coffee from the thermos on his trolley.

Rachel smiled at him. He was singing about sunshine as he moved away, and he certainly did bring sunshine into a room. All of the guests appeared to know him and he had short conversations with each one, complimenting the ladies and joking with the men. Rachel liked the buffet on deck fourteen because it lacked the formality of the reserved restaurants. She had not yet had breakfast in the restaurant for that reason. It was nice to start the day in an informal, albeit frantically busy part of the ship.

After breakfast, she returned to her cabin to collect her camera and a book before going down to deck two to see how Marjorie was. Rachel entered the ward and was relieved to see Marjorie sitting up in bed, wide awake and chatting to Dr Bentley.

"My dear," she smiled at Rachel, "I understand you saved my life yesterday."

"Hardly," replied Rachel. "It was Dr Bentley and his team who did that, but I am so pleased to see you looking better. How are you feeling?"

"A few creaking bones and a bruise on my arm, courtesy of the good doctor here." Marjorie laughed and looked very much like the proud and capable woman Rachel had come to know.

"I'll leave you two to it. I think the patient is back to her formidable self, and I am no match." Dr Bentley smiled. "You will be pleased to know that she has made a full recovery and insists on returning to her stateroom later today, as she says my fees are too high." He walked away laughing, obviously as pleased as Rachel was to see Marjorie well again.

Rachel sat down at the bedside and gave Marjorie a small bunch of dried flowers she had managed to pick up from one of the gift shops on deck five.

"Thank you, my dear," Marjorie said. Rachel noticed that in spite of her good humour, Marjorie was looking tired and drained, with a hint of sadness behind the smile.

"I'm so sorry about yesterday," said Rachel. "It must have been awful for you to witness the accident. I understand the lady was with you at the time?"

"Yes, she was. Her name was Freda McDonald. We had met the day before and were spending the day together. Two old widows – sharing stories of times past." Marjorie's voice faded away and her eyes became watery. "We were about to cross the road and get a taxi back to the ship, when suddenly, I heard the horn—"

Rachel didn't say anything; she was allowing Marjorie to relate the story in her own time and didn't want to interrupt.

"I must have dropped my umbrella. As I saw Freda lying in the road, I realised at once that she was dead. Death is expected at our age, but what a violent way to go—"

Again Marjorie's voice trailed off for a moment while she seemed to be recalling the event.

"She said she wanted to die, you know, to be with her husband."

"Do you think she did it on purpose?" asked Rachel, barely able to comprehend the thought.

"No, I don't. She said that she had contemplated suicide in the past, but that she would never do that to her children and grandchildren. Besides, we had had such a lovely day, and she was laughing and talking."

Rachel was relieved that it was unlikely to have been suicide. "An awful accident then," she concluded.

"It would appear that way," said Marjorie, but she seemed to Rachel to be holding something back.

"Was there anything else?" she probed.

"You'll think I'm a crazy old woman, but I can't seem to shake off the feeling that I am being watched. It started at the beginning of the cruise, and I kept telling myself that it was my imagination because I was travelling without Ralph for the first time. At times, I wondered if it was Ralph watching over me, but as well as not believing in that sort of thing, I feel it's menacing rather than reassuring."

Rachel could hardly breathe. "Go on," she encouraged. "I don't think you're crazy at all; tell me more."

"It sounds odd, I know, but I had the same feeling yesterday in Lisbon. Quite a few times I looked around to see if there was anyone watching me, but apart from lots of faces from the ship, I couldn't find any evidence. The awful thing was that as Freda lay there in the road, I kept thinking it was my fault and that it should have been me instead. And what was worse, I was relieved that it wasn't me – is that terrible? I was filled with terror and shock and couldn't move."

At this point, Marjorie broke down in tears and Rachel gave her a handkerchief.

"It's not terrible to think like that. I think it's quite normal, in fact, to feel a sense of relief mixed with guilt at surviving an incident like the one you experienced. One thing I am certain of though: it wasn't your fault."

"But it was my coat and hat." She almost whispered the words, and the significance of what she was saying finally dawned on Rachel. Remembering seeing Carlos running, she felt sick at the thought of him being involved in this.

Before she could think or say anything more, Sarah entered the ward, smiling.

"It's good to see you two looking well, especially you, Lady Snellthorpe."

It was a relief to change the subject for a while so that Rachel could compose her thoughts, and Marjorie seemed to welcome the break too as they laughed and shared good-humoured banter.

Finally, Sarah said, "Do you mind if I take Rachel away for a minute, Lady Snellthorpe?"

"Of course not," replied Marjorie. "You young things go and chat."

Rachel was reluctant to leave, but something in Sarah's eyes made her think it was important.

"We have had word from the Portuguese police and coroner's office." There was a look of concern on Sarah's face. "They are not certain about this by any means, but a young boy appears to have witnessed Mrs McDonald being pushed into the road by a man in the crowd."

"Could the boy identify the man?" asked Rachel.

"No, apparently not. He was standing close to the elderly ladies, but because of his height and the speed at which it all happened, he only saw the push."

"Is he sure she was pushed?"

"He swears by the story. His parents say he was fascinated by the raindrops rolling down the lady's waterproof coat when it happened. The police believe him, and the coroner says that there is a mark on her back that could have been caused by a push. Without the boy's testimony, he would have put it down to injury from the accident."

"This is terrible," said Rachel. "So it was deliberate?"

"There doesn't seem to be a motive, though. The police say she was unknown to anyone on the ship and are wondering if it was a random killing if it does turn out to be a killing at all. Security on the ship have been informed, but whether the pusher was a passenger or not is unclear."

"Oh, he is on this ship, of that I am certain. And I don't believe she was the intended victim, either."

"What do you mean?"

Rachel explained to Sarah the things that had been nagging her for days: the feeling that she or Marjorie was being watched; the man outside Marjorie's room in the middle of the night; and finally, what she had learned this morning: that Mrs McDonald had been wearing Marjorie's hat and coat.

"You see, they were a similar height and build, and from behind, Mrs McDonald would have looked like Marjorie. I believe she is in danger, but the killer may think that he has got away with murder."

"How so?"

"If he fled the scene, he will believe that Marjorie is dead, and hopefully she will be safe for now."

The only thing that Rachel didn't share was her concern that Carlos might be involved in some way, partly because she did not have a shred of evidence that he was, and partly because she didn't want to think about the possibility.

"We need to let security know. Do you think we should tell Marjorie?"

"It's hard to say, but I think she's been through enough. She already has some inkling that someone is after her, but thinking and knowing are two different things."

"And the reality is, we don't really know at all. It could all be coincidence and the Portuguese boy may just have an overactive imagination. The police aren't actively looking for anyone, but they have let all the ship's captains who were docked that day know that they may have a killer on board. If there is a killer, though, it is much more likely that he is on board this ship rather than any of the others." Sarah paused. "Security has carried out some routine checks and all passengers and crew are back on board, except for poor Mrs McDonald. The problem is, we don't really have a clue what the person might look like. The boy can't even confirm that it was a man who did the pushing!" Sarah looked concerned. "I have to go back to work now because I am on call, but I will catch you later. I will let Dr Bentley know your concerns so that he can alert the captain."

Rachel was left stunned, still finding it difficult to comprehend what might be happening. Now, in addition to her concerns about whether Carlos was involved (something she would investigate herself), she had to work out who might want Marjorie dead, and why.

She went back into the ward area and saw that Marjorie had fallen asleep again. *It must be the sedation*, she thought. *I wonder if I can persuade her to stay another night in the Infirmary.*

Meanwhile, she had work to do. But how do you go about investigating a murder on a cruise ship without any real suspects?

# Chapter 16

Rachel put the telephone down in her room. Marjorie had insisted on being discharged from the ward and was on her way up in a wheelchair. Sarah had called to say that Brigitte was escorting her to her stateroom.

Rachel got up from her bed where she had fallen asleep and noticed that the worry lines were returning to her forehead when she looked in the mirror. *At least this time, it isn't anything to do with Robert.* She could take some comfort from that. She heard talking in the corridor and went out to greet Marjorie.

"They can't keep a good woman down, can they?" Rachel approached Marjorie and gave her a kiss on the cheek.

"I would rather be in my room," replied the old lady, looking tired. Her face was drawn, and although she appeared calm, Rachel noticed she was shaking slightly. Marjorie got up from the wheelchair, and Brigitte said goodbye, mouthing "Look after her" to Rachel. Rachel nodded.

"Thank you, Nurse," said Marjorie.

"Can I help you into your room and get you something to drink?"

"That would be very kind, Rachel, thank you."

They entered the stateroom and found a huge bunch of flowers in a vase on the table, along with a bowl of fruit and a note. Marjorie picked up the note and smiled.

"They must be from Jeremy," she announced, but then Rachel noticed a flicker of disappointment as she read the note. "They are from the captain, how kind of him."

Marjorie handed the note to Rachel.

*"Dear Lady Snellthorpe, wishing you a swift recovery, and may I offer my sincere apologies for your unpleasant experience yesterday. If there is anything I can do, please relay a message via Dr Bentley, who will be keeping an eye on you. Yours sincerely, Captain Peter Jenson."*

Rachel thought it a lovely touch, but she could understand Marjorie's disappointment that her son had not sent her any messages. Not for the first time, Rachel felt a searing anger towards a man she had never met.

"Here you are." Rachel handed her a cup of Earl Grey tea.

"How did you know I like Earl Grey?"
"Observation," replied Rachel. "Is there anything else I can get for you?"

"No thank you, dear. I will eat in my room this evening as I am out on a trip tomorrow in Barcelona." Rachel admired her tenacity and determination to carry on and felt even more protective than ever. "You go out and enjoy yourself. I don't want these unfortunate events to ruin your holiday."

"I'll look in on you tonight if your light is on," said Rachel. "Otherwise I will see you tomorrow after your outing."

Rachel returned to her room and dressed for dinner. For the first formal night on the ship, women donned evening gowns and men wore tuxedos. The captain and all his officers would be present.

As soon as Rachel entered the dining room, she felt an arm rest on her shoulder. She turned to see Carlos beaming down at her and she felt familiar butterflies in her stomach. *Don't fall under his spell,* she warned herself, without much success.

"You look breathtakingly beautiful tonight," he said as he held her apart from him and gave her an appraising look up and down. She had on a red strapless evening gown with a matching bow above the left breast, and even with her wrap covering her shoulders, she was attracting appreciative glances from other men as they entered the dining room.

Her blue eyes shone as she smiled and relaxed for the first time that day. Carlos looked incredibly handsome in his tuxedo, and he was annoyingly confident and assured as he took her arm and led her to their table.

Dinner passed pleasantly. No-one at the table seemed to know about the events that had unfolded the day before, except perhaps Carlos. He kept giving Rachel looks as though he wanted to say something, but then changed his mind.

For her part, Rachel tried to probe him with questions about where he was from and what he did, but he was evasive. In between, he was charming, and his commanding presence meant that the others on the table wanted to speak with him just as much as she did.

*So much for being skilled at information gathering.* It was much easier when Rachel was questioning suspects or victims because she could be more frank.

After dinner, Carlos escorted her to the main atrium to meet with the captain and his officers. They were handed a glass of champagne, and Rachel was feeling a lot more at ease, partly because she had already had two glasses of wine with dinner, and now the champagne was filling her stomach with a warm, pleasant glow. She wasn't used to drinking in quantities and her head was swimming. Carlos was more attentive than he had been thus far in the cruise, and she was enjoying his closeness.

Then she abruptly remembered her suspicions.

"Did you enjoy yourself yesterday?" she asked.

"In Lisbon?" He didn't wait for her to acknowledge this. "It was alright. I went into town that was all. I have been to Lisbon many times before."

"Oh, I see. Did you not visit the western end of the harbour?"

"No, I returned to the ship from town." Rachel noticed a brief hesitation and a flicker of his eyes before he answered. Just enough to tell her he was lying.
Rachel stiffened slightly.

"I'm tired, I need to go to bed," she said, suddenly turning away. He grabbed her hand and pulled her towards him, and she felt breathless as he looked into her eyes.

"I will see you tomorrow," he whispered and kissed her lightly on the lips. Rachel summoned all of her willpower and strength in order to prevent this becoming a deeper kiss and broke away for the second time.

"Goodnight," she mumbled and left the atrium.

She didn't return to her room immediately. Deciding to get some fresh air first, she took a walk around one of the upper decks. She passed the outdoor movie screen and noticed that a film was showing, but she didn't stop to watch.

Her thoughts were confused. If it were not for the Marjorie thing, she would be enjoying her time with Carlos much more, but the nagging doubts in her head kept her from trusting him.

After about an hour of staring out to sea, Rachel returned to her stateroom. Marjorie's light was out, so she went straight to bed, and immediately her head hit the pillow, she was wrapped in dreams concerning romance and murder.

Rachel woke at seven the next morning after a restless night and saw that the ship was docked in Barcelona. Knowing that Sarah was working, Rachel had booked herself on to one of the coach tours to Montserrat for the morning, and afterwards she would meet Sarah to go to Las Ramblas for some shopping.

As she opened her door, she saw Josie in the corridor. "Good morning, ma'am Rachel," the Philippine woman said.

"Good morning, Josie. Have you seen Lady Snellthorpe this morning?"

"Yes, ma'am, she left early to go on her outing. Dr Bentley visited her and escorted her to her meeting area."

Rachel was relieved. "See you later."

"Have a nice day, ma'am Rachel," said Josie as she entered one of the staterooms armed with new bed linen and towels.

Rachel walked up the corridor towards the theatre where she would be meeting her tour guide. She was given a blue sticker with a number nine printed on it, indicating which tour group she would join, and then she sat and waited patiently until her number was called.

The group followed one of the crew members down to deck four where they passed through the usual security before leaving via a ramp down to the port side. The others in the group had obviously done this before, and

Rachel followed them to a coach with a large number nine sign displayed in the window. The passengers were all greeted by a Spanish woman, who introduced herself as Maria, and the coach driver called Patrick.

Once on the coach, Rachel found a seat. It wasn't long before an Asian family sat around her, a teenager sitting next to Rachel.

"Hi, I'm Vindra," the girl said. "You're very pretty."

"I'm Rachel," she replied, laughing. "And so are you!"

Vindra was thirteen going on twenty, and turned out to be a chatty, outgoing young girl who entertained Rachel with stories of her school-life in Kent.

"If she annoys you, tell her to shut up," said the woman on the seats parallel to theirs. Rachel noticed she had much more of an accent than Vindra and wore a beautiful blue sari. *Silk*, Rachel thought. *She must be quite hot.* Sitting next to her was a man who appeared to be in his forties, wearing a smart short-sleeved white shirt and brown trousers.

"She is not annoying me," said Rachel, politely.

Vindra was dressed less formally than her parents, wearing pink shorts to mid-thigh and a vest with the word 'Lisbon' sprawled across the front. She smiled at Rachel, a beautiful smile that showed off her white teeth, and her deep brown eyes shone.

*You are going to be a heartbreaker.*

Rachel enjoyed the chatter and listened to the family as they laughed together. On the seat in front of Vindra's parents were two young boys who, Vindra told her, were six and eight. They were playing video games from what Rachel could make out.

"They would be searching for Pokémons if they had mobile phones, but Dad won't let them have one yet because they are too young," explained Vindra. "I do let them use mine, but Dad told me off in Lisbon because they kept getting in people's way while they were chasing after the Pokémons."

The guide drew the passengers' attention to the various landmarks on the drive up to Montserrat. The Benedictine Monastery was perched on the mountainside with spectacular views. Once the coach stopped, Rachel parted with the group and decided to go for a wander by herself.

The monastery was spectacular to look at, and she admired the basilica which the guide had said was Romanesque. In spite of the number of people there, Rachel thought how peaceful it appeared, and she admired those who lived, worked and prayed there.

She caught sight of some of the monks and followed them into the main building. Here she found beautiful architecture and evidence of a life that had not changed in centuries. She sat for a while and enjoyed the peace and tranquillity until a group of tourists arrived with a tour guide who had a rather loud voice. Rachel watched the group for a short time and realised the guide was speaking French. Rachel had studied the language at school to A level and was able to hold a relatively fluent conversation, but she was struggling to make out some of the guide's words. They were probably technical, relating to the architecture around her.

She left the monastery and headed in to the main plaza where the shops were situated. Ordering a cup of coffee from an outside café area, she watched as people crowded into the small souvenir shops. There were a number of tour groups visiting, some from her ship and some from another cruise ship she had seen in the port. The Mediterranean was busy at this time of year and tourism brought a welcome boost to the Spanish economy, which was not in the healthiest of conditions.

Rachel joined the rest of her group for lunch, provided as part of the tour package, and Vindra insisted she join her and her family to eat. Rachel liked this girl and was pleased that her parents allowed her to express herself so openly. She had met some Asian parents through her line of work who baulked at their children becoming a part of the western culture and still encouraged arranged marriages. Vindra had explained to Rachel on the coach that her father was a strict Hindu, but that he had agreed to allow his children to choose their own marriage partners.

"He would prefer them to be Asian," Vindra said, "but will accept them, whoever they are."

Rachel acknowledged the difficulties of integration into western culture for those who had not been brought up in the West, and understood the concerns of parents as her own parents found some aspects of western life difficult, too. Having a vicar as a father, she sometimes felt she was more aligned to the morals of other cultures than her own. Even though her brother had renounced Christianity and lived with his girlfriend, Amy, Rachel's parents still welcomed Amy and her daughter from a previous relationship into their home.

"Life's complicated," her father had said. "We are not here to judge people, but to live as honestly before God as we can."

Rachel agreed with this sentiment, and although she knew what she believed, she understood that for many, her way of life was archaic.

She was brought out of her reverie by Vindra.

"Rachel, come on! It's time to go back to the bus."

With that, Vindra took Rachel's hand as though leading a small child back to the coach.

Vindra continued her nattering all the way back to the cruise terminal, and Rachel half listened and half dozed through the journey.

Sarah was waiting for her as she got off the coach.

"Looks like you had fun," Sarah said, smiling.

"I did, actually. Vindra is entertaining and beautiful, inside and out. I hope she stays that way."

"Well, come on, you. It's time to go to Las Ramblas. Remember to hang on to your bag as there are a lot of thieves around, but it is quite spectacular. You will love the stalls and the cafés."

"You forget I am trained in self-defence and have a black belt in Karate."

"I did forget, sorry. I feel much safer now."

Sarah took Rachel's arm, and they began their walk.

The temperature was 30 degrees centigrade as they entered Las Ramblas, and Rachel loved it immediately. Stalls flanked both sides of the road, selling various wares. Cafés were also on both sides of the road, and outdoor seating areas were set up all along the centre so that people could stop at any time they wanted to for a drink or food.

"Look at him!" Rachel exclaimed as she saw a man dressed in a skin-tight suit, painted gold and balancing upside-down on one hand, staying absolutely still.

"Human statues," remarked Sarah. "People have their photos taken beside them and put money into the caps or containers. Look, there's someone doing just that."

Rachel watched a child standing next to the man while his mum took a photo on her mobile phone. The child then put some coins into the man's gold top hat.

"It makes a change from busking," said Sarah.

"Indeed it does. Oh, I do like it here, Sarah."

"I knew you would. Come on, let's keep walking."

The two young women spent a pleasant couple of hours wandering up and down Las Ramblas, and Rachel bought a Barcelona tea towel for her mum and a pair of brightly coloured socks for her dad with a picture of Barcelona's football stadium sewn into them. It was only when they sat down to have coffee and ice cream that they discussed the events of the past few days.

"Graham did decide to alert the captain to your suspicions, and the captain was aware of the report given by the Portuguese police, but there is not much else that can be done. The captain and Graham agree with your view that the killer, if there is one, believes he has been successful and that Marjorie should be safe."

"I do hope so," replied Rachel. "But what if he sees her?"

*And what if Carlos is involved?* She kept that thought to herself.

"The Captain has alerted security but they have nothing to go on. No description and no real evidence that it was a murder at all when it comes down to it."

"You're right, it could all just be a nasty sequence of coincidences, I suppose." Rachel hoped rather than believed this to be true.

"He has also assigned a security officer to keep an eye out for Marjorie, but it will be difficult because they have so much to do with actual disturbances that go on throughout the ship. They had to arrest someone last night and found cocaine in his luggage. Thankfully only for personal use, but we do get drugs on board as we can't search all the passengers' luggage."

By the time Rachel returned to the ship, she felt quite calm. Sarah went back to work and Rachel went and sat on her balcony. The late afternoon sun glittered, and Rachel dreamily enjoyed the weather while watching the coaches returning way down below her.

It was getting close to sail away time when she saw what she assumed were the final two coaches arriving. She watched as passengers got off and became alert when she saw Marjorie being assisted from the penultimate coach. Rachel was pleased that Marjorie had made it out for the day and watched as she stood upright.

She was about to look away when, to her horror, she saw Carlos get off of the same coach about ten people behind Marjorie. Reaching for her binoculars, Rachel focussed the lenses on him. It was hard to see whether he was following Marjorie or whether this was yet another coincidence.

Rachel put the glasses down as her heart sank into the pit of her stomach and her head throbbed. Had she been right to be suspicious of Carlos?

*Dear God, no!* she pleaded.

# Chapter 17

The man was livid when he got back to the ship. He had gone on land to check his bank account, but no money had been added. He had then spent most of the day trying to get his mobile phone to work. It was a burner phone he had picked up a day before the cruise so that it couldn't be traced, but the damn thing wasn't working.

*I'll kill that stupid man when I get hold of him.*

Then he caught sight of the woman and couldn't believe his eyes. He joined the coach trip she was on, bribing the driver, and confirmed it was her. How had she survived?

It gradually dawned on him that he had killed the wrong woman and he felt a knot in his stomach. He had relaxed for the past couple of days as the adrenaline had subsided and he had started to let his guard down again. He always liked to celebrate his kills with a woman and he had just the one in mind. He couldn't believe his bad luck.

When he got back to the ship, he was angry, but from his calm outward demeanour, nobody would have known it. Years of preparation and training as a hitman had given him the ability to hide his feelings beneath an outwardly charming facade. After his first kill at the age of seventeen, when he had been sick for two weeks, he had been determined that this would never happen again, and he had trained himself well. He kept to a rigid routine of exercise and mental discipline, teaching himself to behave perfectly normally, even moments after a kill.

He wasn't keen on killing a woman in her eighties, and now he had killed another one by accident. This had never happened before. Doubts about this job plagued him again. It wasn't his normal hit, and he had been in two minds about taking it, but money was tight and he needed the work. A killer always needed to stay in practise; he'd heard of others who lost the edge when they had big gaps in-between jobs. He was stashing money away so that he could retire at forty because he didn't want to be in the killing game for ever. It wasn't something he took pleasure in, but he did take a certain pride in his work, and he had never failed an assignment before.

The mobile signal was working again; it had been off all day, in spite of his being on land. He looked at the screen: sixteen missed calls. Blast! Well, at least he knew what this was all about.

He was about to do a call back when the phone rang in his hand. Cursing to himself, he answered.

"You damn well missed her, you idiot. You said it was done! I've been trying to get you for two days."

"Calm down, will you. I saw her today, so I realised. What happened?"

"You tell me!" The shouting continued down the phone. "You killed the wrong woman. What kind of killer are you? You need to get this done, and it needs to look like an accident, which might prove difficult now. Do they suspect anything?"

"No, no. I heard the crew talking when I got back to the ship the other day and they said there had been an accident. It's fine, no-one suspects. I will do it, but I need to leave it a few days for the memory of the other one to die down, just in case. There's still plenty of time."

"Make sure you do and text me when it's done. No mistakes this time. Remember to use this number."

The man on the other end of the line hung up; he hadn't even sounded concerned that someone else had been killed.

*Well, if he doesn't care, I certainly don't. I'm not in the business of caring, but I guess I am going to have to pull back a bit on the relationship that I've been developing. Just when things were starting to get interesting.*

He made his way down to the bar and ordered a brandy before starting his planning.

*This one would have to be different.*

# Chapter 18

Marjorie enjoyed a pleasant day out on the coach tour although she couldn't help thinking about Freda and how her family must be feeling. There was also the nagging doubt that perhaps Freda had been pushed, and if so – who would want to do such a thing? The concern about the fact that Freda had been wearing her hat and coat had subsided somewhat as Marjorie persuaded herself that there was no way she could have been the intended victim. She mulled over in her mind whether anyone would want her killed and the idea was preposterous. Although Jeremy stood to inherit everything when she died, the business had always been profitable, giving him a very generous salary and bonuses.

Marjorie had tried really hard to dispel all of these thoughts from her mind, and she felt the tears falling down her cheeks as she wished Ralph was still alive. He would have known exactly what was going on and would have reassured her that she had just witnessed a terrible accident and was in shock. This made her feel better as she felt the warmth of Ralph sitting next to her once again, whispering words of comfort. Sometimes the pain of losing him was too much to bear. Freda had understood that, and the only consolation that Marjorie could gain from the tragedy was that Freda was now with her beloved husband.

Not being one to dwell in self-pity, Marjorie resolved to pull herself together. Ralph had made her promise that she would make the best of life if he departed before her and said he would be keeping an eye on her from above to make sure she did, and she smiled at the thought. The coach tour guide was starting to explain exactly where they were on their journey and she put the headphones on to listen.

The tour took in the Olympic Ring on the outskirts of the city before heading on to Gaudí's unfinished masterpiece, the cathedral. Most of the tour involved sitting and listening, which was all Marjorie could manage today anyway because her bones still ached from the hypothermia she had experienced. Dr Bentley had not wanted her to go on a tour at all today, but she had persuaded him to let her in spite of his reservations.

Everyone had been so kind, and if it had not been for Rachel, she didn't know what would have become of her. Spending time with Rachel had renewed her faith in young people; she was such a kind and caring girl, and the sadness that had been in her eyes at the start of the cruise had started to dissipate. Marjorie was determined that Rachel should be allowed to enjoy her holiday and she didn't want her feeling that she needed to look after a silly old woman who had got herself into a fix.

The guide was talking about thousands of years of Barcelona history and famous sights such as monasteries and basilicas when Marjorie drifted off to sleep. She was brought to a sudden awakening when the coach stopped, and as she opened her eyes, she saw that they were back at the ship. The tour guide helped her to her feet as she had stiffened up a little and the driver lifted her down the steps onto the ground. Marjorie gave them both a gratuity and thanked them for the tour before one of the crew members arrived to escort her back on board the *Coral Queen*.

"Did you have a nice trip, ma'am?" he asked as he handed her an iced flannel to refresh herself with, followed by a cool drink of squash.

"Yes, thank you, it was interesting."

"I will accompany you on board, madam."
Marjorie looked at the smart man who offered her his arm, detecting an Australian accent.

"There's really no need," she replied. "I can manage."

"Doctor's orders, madam."

"Oh well, in that case." Marjorie gratefully took the young man's arm and was pleased of the support as she was starting to feel a little lightheaded. These dizzy spells had worsened since she'd been in the hospital ward, and she wasn't sure whether they were a normal reaction to what she had experienced or something else. She hadn't yet mentioned them to anyone, but thought she might need to if they continued.

Once she was safely back on board ship, she was escorted all the way to her stateroom where she ordered a pot of coffee as she was too tired to make tea. The stateroom had been cleaned and left looking immaculate by Josie, who had topped up the tea supplies. It had been another very hot day, and she was pleased to be in her air-conditioned room.

The telephone rang in her room.

"Hello, Mother." She heard Jeremy's voice at the other end. "I understand you have been unwell."

His tone was crisp and to the point. "Yes, it was an awful event. I met a friend on board and she fell into the road and was run over. I was in shock and they say I suffered hypothermia."

"Well I hope you will be more careful in the future, Mother. Are you well now?"

"Yes, I am much better, thank you. There was a lovely girl—"

"Sorry, Mother. I can't speak for long. I have to go into a meeting. Enjoy the rest of your cruise. Bye."

"Bye, I love you." She knew he had hung up before she finished.

*Oh well, at least he called.*

# Chapter 19

It had been six days since Freda had died and Rachel was beginning to put it to the back of her mind, deciding it was just an unfortunate accident after all. The doctor and the captain had arrived at the same conclusion and everybody was more relaxed.

That afternoon, Sarah had explained to Rachel that the Portuguese police had allowed Freda's body to be released for repatriation to Scotland, also concluding that it had been an accidental death. They could not confirm the boy's story, and none of the other witnesses had seen anything sinister or suspicious.

"It looks like the boy had an overactive imagination after all."

"Yes, I'm sure you're right," agreed Rachel. "Marjorie seems much happier in herself, too. She says she has been feeling jittery since her husband died and the accident sent her into shock."

"Well, the captain has had her followed for the past five days since she left the infirmary and nothing suspicious has been spotted by the undercover crew members, so he has called them off."

"Did Marjorie know?"

"No, no-one knew, not even Graham. The captain kept it all very hush-hush until he was sure that she wasn't being followed. They checked off all the passengers on the same trips, and apart from a family from Ontario, there was no overlap. The poor family has been police checked and everything, and there are no links to the UK at all, let alone to Lady Snellthorpe or her family."

"That's wonderful news," Rachel said.

"Now you can concentrate on that dishy Italian, at last!" Sarah laughed. "I've got a date myself tonight with the deputy head of security. We got to know each other when I had to explain what had happened to Marjorie."

"You kept that under your belt." Rachel giggled.

"It only happened today. Hot off the press, and you are the first to know, of course."

Rachel had left Sarah to go and get ready for her evening and had stopped in on Marjorie before returning to her own room. They were ten days into the cruise and nothing further had caused any concerns. Marjorie's son had phoned her twice, and this seemed to please the old lady, although Rachel still got the impression they were not overly close.

Rachel beamed at the thought of seeing Carlos. As Marjorie seemed so much happier, she could now unwind and enjoy her time with Carlos without suspecting him of any wrong-doing. She had only managed to spend a little bit of time with him over the past few days as he had been distracted.

"Work stuff," he had explained when she'd asked. However, this evening, he was taking her to the theatre after dinner.

She was excited and nervous at the prospect of spending some time with Carlos after the evening meal. Choosing a casual cotton summer dress with short sleeves, she put on a pair of white sling-back sandals. Her skin was starting to look tanned, and it gave her a healthy glow. She spent time applying a thin layer of makeup that complemented her features, and she was pleased with the result.

Carlos was waiting for her outside the dining room and he escorted her to the now familiar table. Conversation flowed freely as each of the dinner companions had developed a familiar, relaxed camaraderie. Sue and Greg had been initially reserved, but even they engaged in quips and teases at the table.

Jean looked at Rachel. "Beautiful as ever," she remarked and Rachel blushed as she felt all eyes move towards her. She bore her beauty in a reserved way and didn't think about it until people brought it to her attention.

She changed the subject. "Have you been off ship today?" The ship had been docked at the island of

Corsica, and was now on the way to the final stop before the return home, Gibraltar.

Jean and Brenda didn't usually venture too far from the ship as they liked to be close by. Brenda suffered from health anxiety, and although she was making progress, she still found new places difficult to explore in a totally relaxed way. Jean appeared to accept this and was supportive of her friend.

It was Brenda who replied. "Yes, we did today. We went on a tour to an aromatherapy craft factory and then went on to a vineyard for wine tasting and ate locally made nougat."

"Oh, I am envious," Florence chipped in. "We nearly went on that trip, but we went for a walk around the old town by ourselves today. David said he couldn't take another coach tour."

Florence gave David a pretend glare, and he squeezed her arm.

"Sorry, love, next time."

The dining room was busy this evening, and Stavros and Geraldine were rushed off their feet. Lobster was on the menu, and most of those at Table 305 chose that as the main course.

"I think we will all be needing to shape up when we get back home," said Greg as he watched his wife finish up her dessert. Sue had a healthy appetite, and Greg reminded her of it frequently, which Rachel had found embarrassing at times. Sue actually took no notice of him whatsoever in this regard and chomped her way through as much food as was laid on the table.

As dinner finished, each couple gradually dispersed, leaving Carlos and Rachel alone together, finishing an after-dinner cappuccino.

"It is nice to have you to myself for a while," said Carlos as he gazed into her eyes.

Rachel liked having his attention, and although she wanted the relationship to develop, she still had reservations about a holiday fling and where it would lead. There was also a much smaller, but still nagging doubt about who this man was. He gave nothing away, and even exercising all her womanly charm, she barely knew anything about him. He said he wanted to forget about life on shore and enjoy the moment. Above all else, Rachel feared he was married. She had almost cleared him of any involvement with Marjorie, but if he was married, that would explain his secrecy.

Rachel decided that although she wanted to enjoy this night, she had to find out more about this man if they were to become anything other than friends. She opened her mouth to ask him, but before she got the opportunity, he leaned in towards her and kissed her lightly on the lips. She pulled away slightly, aware of waiters and other diners still in the vicinity.

"What's the matter?" he asked.

"Please don't do that," she responded, knowing that she was sounding silly and her voice had taken on a slightly higher pitch. She turned, took her shawl from the back of the chair and walked away before he had the opportunity to move.

Once outside the restaurant, she picked up her pace until she found herself running towards the upper decks.

"Rachel, stop!" She heard his voice at a distance behind her. Once she arrived on deck twelve, she stopped and gazed out to sea, not knowing what on earth had got into her.

*Well, that was mature!* she scolded herself. *I'm just not ready.*

She finally acknowledged that her problem was still Robert and the unwelcome fact that he had shattered her trust in men. Facing up to this reality, she leaned over the ship's rail and cried a deep, sobbing cry that released some of the excruciating pain that she had been bottling up for months. A few people passed by and discreetly looked away, continuing on with their night-time strolls.

After crying for about an hour, she began to feel calm again. All these weeks, she had been throwing herself into her work, trying to avoid the inevitable chasm of emptiness and pain that was like a boil that had to be burst before it could heal. Meeting Carlos had been wonderful, she acknowledged, but it had also made her face up to the lack of trust she now had towards the opposite sex. Fearing he might be married added to the dilemma. She enjoyed his attention, and when he kissed her, it sent electric shocks through her body, but was it all a show?

*Would he turn out to be another Robert?*

She didn't even know what he believed. How would he feel about her religion? Would he understand? Did he believe in God? Most of all, though, it was the anger and misery that Robert had caused that tormented her.

"I hate you, Robert," she shouted. "I was ready to give my life to you, you're a contemptible rat. You behaved shamefully, and I hope you live in misery for the rest of your life."

Her words were lost in the night sky, and the noise of the waves drowned them out. Rachel stopped, shocked at the vehemence she'd felt in her heart – that gentle heart that had been so easily broken. These were not nice feelings. She was having visions of some of the people she had arrested who had shouted and cursed and sworn, giving off nothing but anger.

She settled herself.

*I cannot go there, but I cannot give my heart away so easily again. I must protect it at all costs.*

She stood upright, lifted her head and walked back towards her stateroom, determined to put Carlos out of her head before she made a huge mistake.

Deciding to walk to the bow of the ship, she went down the most forward steps to avoid the crowds who tended to use the centre stair and lift areas as they gave easier access to all of the entertainment areas. It was dark as she made her way down the outer steps first before going inside to descend to deck nine. As she walked along the corridor towards her stateroom, she had the feeling of being watched again, but there was no-one in sight. Josie's assistant came out of one of the staterooms and Rachel nodded to him, keeping her head down so that he couldn't see she had been crying.

When she entered her stateroom, she found the balcony doors open, which was unusual. *Josie must have left them open by mistake.* Walking out onto the balcony as it was a nice, warm evening, and the sky was clear, she could hear noises coming from Marjorie's room next door and called out. The balcony screens were such that she couldn't see into Marjorie's room unless she peered round from the front, which she only did when she knew Marjorie was on the balcony.

"Good evening, Marjorie," Rachel shouted, but there was no reply. Perhaps she was going to bed, and it was difficult to hear above the waves. Rachel decided to call it a night and went back into her stateroom.

An hour later, she awoke as she thought she heard Marjorie's door close and movement next door. Rachel got up and dressed quickly into a pair of slacks before knocking at her neighbour's door.

"Good evening, my dear." Marjorie was fully dressed and looking a little flushed.

"Good evening. Erm, I just thought I would check in on you. Have you been out?"

"Come in, dear. Yes, I went to the theatre with Mr and Mrs Hutchinson, a couple I met on one of my trips. They are really sweet – from Dallas, you know."

Rachel was feeling an uncomfortable adrenaline surge again as she entered the room. She noticed the balcony doors were closed, and the room looked untouched since it had been made up by the stewards earlier.

"Are you alright, Rachel?" Marjorie was staring at her.

"Yes, sorry. I was asleep, I think I must have heard you and wanted to say goodnight. I will leave you to it, then." Rachel turned to go, but then she noticed there were tablets on the table at the side of Marjorie's bed. "Are those your painkillers? I almost forgot, Sarah asked me to swap them for slightly weaker ones." Rachel had no idea why she was saying this, but she grabbed the pills before Marjorie could object. "I think I left them down in the medical centre, I'll go and get them for you."

With that, she turned and rushed down to deck two. There was no-one there, and the area was closed off, but Rachel could see a light coming from the infirmary so she knocked.

Bernard answered. "Hello, Rachel, Sarah's off tonight," he said in his Philippine accent. "Hot date!"

"Oh yes, sorry, I forgot. Do you have any paracetamol? I seem to have run out and I've got a splitting headache."

"Are you alright? You look like you've seen a ghost."

"I'm fine, just a bad head."

"I'll go and get you some tablets."

Bernard came back with a full packet of paracetamol tablets. "Do you want me to label them for you?"

"No, it's okay, I know what to do, thanks. Please bill them to my room."

Rachel went back to Marjorie's stateroom and gave her the paracetamol before leaving a rather confused looking lady staring after her. When she got back to her own room, she stared at the tablets she had taken from Marjorie, but they made no impression on her. One tablet looked like another, except illegal drugs, which she was pretty good at spotting.

She sat on her bed, thinking about what she should do now. There had definitely been someone in Marjorie's room earlier, and it hadn't been Marjorie. It wasn't the assistant steward either because she had seen him further down the corridor. The only other person with a legitimate reason to be there would have been Josie, and if it was not her, then who?

Rachel tucked the tablets into her bedside cupboard and decided that she would ask Josie in the morning if she had been making up Marjorie's room later than usual. As she drifted off to sleep, Rachel really did start to develop a headache and wished she had kept some of the paracetamol for herself. Thoughts whirred around in her head again, including visions of Robert and Carlos.

The next morning, Rachel woke early and decided to catch Josie before going for a run. She went into the corridor and saw a different steward, a stocky Asian man who smiled pleasantly.

"Good morning, ma'am."

"Good morning, I was looking for Josie."

"Sorry, ma'am, Josie burned hand last night. Gone help elsewhere. I help, ma'am?"

"No, thank you. It's alright, it wasn't important."

Her headache was returning. *Drat!*

She headed upstairs for her run, joining her singing Jamaican friend from the breakfast buffet as he ran at the same time most mornings. He usually made her smile, but today she was deep in thought, mulling over the events of the previous night. She wished she had her police uniform on so that she could ask questions formally, but that wasn't to be. The reassuring thought was that it was most likely to have been Josie in Marjorie's room rather than anyone else, and the worst that could happen would be that Rachel would look rather foolish having taken away the painkillers.

*Daylight and running always help clear the head,* she thought as she returned to her stateroom for a shower.

# Chapter 20

Rachel took Marjorie's tablets to the medical centre shortly after breakfast and asked Dr Bentley to check them.

"There's nothing wrong with the tablets, these are the ones I prescribed." He looked perplexed. "What made you think there was a problem?"

Rachel explained about hearing noises in Marjorie's stateroom the night before and how she had initially thought it was the old lady herself. She explained about being woken up later when Marjorie had arrived back and how she had managed to remove the tablets with a cock and bull story about milder painkillers.

Dr Bentley frowned. "Look, you had a shock early on in the cruise and your mind is still coping with the fact that it was just a tragic accident. In the meantime, your policewoman mind-set is seeing villains behind every door where there are none. When I started medicine, I was the same – every pain was cancer. Every symptom more serious than it actually was, and I developed a warped view of the world where everyone was seriously ill. But this was *my* world, not the real one."

It made sense. Rachel knew that her senses were in overdrive, and the stress of the broken engagement had made her work and study even harder than ever, immersing herself in criminology books. The accident early on in the cruise had re-awoken her senses, and she was just beginning to relax when the issue with Carlos had triggered another stress reaction.

"How do I learn to deal with it?" she asked.

"It takes time." Dr Bentley got up to leave as Sarah entered the clinic room with a cup of coffee. "You were suddenly awoken last night and your mind was overactive after hearing the noises earlier. You reacted, end of story. If it had been a crime scene, you would have saved the old dear's life, but it wasn't. No harm done."

Dr Bentley left the room.

"Sometimes I think I'm going mad," Rachel confided in Sarah.

"There's no-one I know who is saner," said her friend. "Come on, drink up, there's no need to worry. Apart from last night, you have been more yourself. Just put it down to experience."

"You're right, I guess all I've hurt is my pride. Thank goodness your Dr Bentley is so understanding. He didn't even tell me off about switching the pills."

"Those painkillers would be too strong now, anyway. They probably made her sleepy, so it was a good switch."

Rachel felt pleased that everything had been put into perspective. She made a note to herself to fit in some relaxation classes when she got back to work.

Sarah stood up. "I'd better get back to work. Are we still on for Gibraltar tomorrow?"

"Yes, but I don't know how you persuaded me to join you on the Barbary ape trip. I hate monkeys, and I hear these ones can be quite aggressive."

"I know, but I'm fascinated by nature, you know that. See you tomorrow in the atrium."

As Sarah went back to the waiting room to call her next patient through, Rachel returned to her stateroom to change into shorts before going to the upper deck in search of light entertainment and food. Deck fourteen was packed as ever with people sunbathing and swimming, but she managed to find a sunbed and made herself comfortable, stripping down to her bikini. Her skin glistened in the sun as she applied sun cream and she was pleased to see that her usually pale skin had developed a nice bronzed glow. She was always careful in the sun as she was prone to burning, and a childhood experience of painful blistering had taught her a lifelong lesson. She was also well aware of the risks of skin cancer from the sun's harmful rays, and this was an added incentive to apply frequent dollops of sun cream.

Rachel looked around, and all she could see were people and sunbeds. Children were swimming, and some people had chosen beds in the shade. Looking out to sea, she could see that the Mediterranean was beautifully calm and blue. There was something therapeutic about the way the ship bobbed gently up and down as it made its way in a westerly direction towards Gibraltar.

She was looking forward to visiting this headland of which her grandfather had spoken. He had been stationed in Gibraltar during the war and spoke fondly of what he called Mediterranean England. The colony still belonged to the United Kingdom, a fact which was occasionally under dispute by the Spanish who wanted to reclaim it.

Rachel pulled a book out from her bag and decided to spend some time reading. This was a pleasure she had largely given up as the majority of her reading in recent years had been textbooks or policing manuals. It was nice to read something completely different. She was avoiding romantic novels, and had picked up a crime thriller by Dee Henderson, an author she had discovered on a recommendation from Louise, Robert's sister. Many of the people in her books were broken for one reason or another, but they managed to find happiness and purpose through their work and relationships. Maybe there was hope for Rachel yet.

In spite of the buzz of activity all around her, Rachel managed to get lost in a fictional world for a while, but now she was hungry. She decided to do what everybody else did and leave her towel while she went into the buffet dining room to collect some lunch. Craving healthy food, she opted for a large bowl of Mediterranean salad.

Having gathered her salad, she was just about to make her way back outside to her sunbed when she saw a familiar figure in the pizza queue. Carlos looked as handsome as ever, and Rachel debated whether to avoid him or apologise for the previous evening. The decision was made for her as Carlos turned his head and saw her standing there. He left the queue and joined her.

"What the heck happened last night?" He sounded confused rather than angry, so she tried to explain.

"I'm sorry, I am just not ready for a relationship at the moment, and I don't do one-night stands."

"Okay, I understand. I can't say they are my cup of tea either, but can we be friends and see where things lead?"

His brown eyes were piercing her with an intensity that she had not seen before and he seemed genuinely relieved when she answered positively.

"Right, don't go anywhere. I will get a pizza and we can relax together."

Rachel waited, not sure whether this was a good idea because she was struggling with her feelings for this man. There was something mysterious about him, the way he wouldn't talk about himself or what he did for a living, and yet he had just shown a vulnerability which she hadn't seen before. It was new, and attractive. He was drop-dead gorgeous, as her friends would say, yet he was also interesting and able to converse on many different levels. She was drawn to him, and this could prove dangerous if she dropped her guard but having decided that she was not ready for a relationship, she would summon all her self-control to make sure that she was not put in a position of compromise.

Carlos rejoined her and they walked out to where she had been lying on a sunbed. He perched himself on the side of the bed and they chatted as if nothing untoward had happened. Ordering cocktails from one of the waiters who was passing, Carlos handed her a sangria. The drink was loaded with ice, and she found it refreshing as she felt it on the back of her throat.

She loosened up as they continued to chat for a while. Rachel found it quite distracting when he took his shirt and shorts off and sat in his swimming trunks on the edge of her bed. Close up, he was a lot more muscular than she had previously thought, and his biceps were firm.

"Look, there's a free bed." She pointed it out as someone got up on her left-hand side. He smiled at her teasingly as he moved over to the bed next to her and appeared fully aware of the effect he was having on her. Rachel felt completely relaxed now. Was it the sangria or was it the Mediterranean sun that was helping her to laugh again?

Carlos looked at his watch. "I need to go now, but I will see you at dinner later. Yes?"

Rachel felt slightly disappointed, but nodded. She watched him go and then decided to move herself as the afternoon was turning into evening.

She was collecting her things together when she saw Marjorie.

"Hello," she said.

"Oh hello, Rachel. It's very hot out here, isn't it? I was just going to head back to my room and dress for dinner."

"Me too." Rachel smiled and took the old lady's arm.

"Let's go together."

# Chapter 21

He was bitterly disappointed not to have finished the job completely so that he could relax and enjoy time with the girl he had met. Having made his way into the woman's stateroom, all he'd had to do was wait until she returned. He could have had her over the side in seconds.

It had been planned down to the last detail. He'd waited until the cabin stewards had gone into the rooms, then he had managed to sneak into the room next door while the steward was collecting supplies to replenish teas. Hiding behind the curtains that were already drawn, he had waited for the steward to close the door before opening the balcony doors.

He was about to close them when he heard someone coming into the room. He mustn't be seen. Quick to react, he climbed over the rail and onto the old woman's balcony. He had gone in earlier and unlocked the doors while the steward had been cleaning the bathroom, but the curtains were still open so he couldn't hide.

He tripped over a table on his way into the room, then heard a woman's voice call out, so he closed the balcony doors quickly. Annoyed that he had been heard, he decided it was too risky to make the murder look like an accidental fall overboard.

*I'll have to come up with another plan now.*

His employer was becoming impatient and had called again when the ship was docked in Corsica. He had explained it would all be done by the time the ship got to Gibraltar and he would call from there.

*It has to be tonight, then. I have to finish the job tonight so that I can get paid and get this ridiculous man off my back.*

He couldn't believe how difficult it was to kill off an old woman, who appeared to have more lives than a cat. Not for the first time, he considered reneging on the job, but this was not possible. His reputation would be tarnished and no-one would hire him again. These things had a way of getting around, and he didn't want rumours spreading that he couldn't finish off a woman in her eighties – he would be the laughing stock. Being a hired killer was all about reputation, and competence and efficiency were key to maintaining a reputation and guaranteeing future hires.

He had taken this job on the back of a kill in the Alps that he had made look like a skiing accident. Delighted with the result of that job, he smiled as he remembered it. It had been successfully completed on the second day of the trip, and he had enjoyed a holiday as soon as it was over.

Luck had been with him that day. He'd heard his target storming out of the hotel early in the morning after a violent row with his wife and had no qualms about killing the man. In fact, he was looking forward to it as he couldn't abide men who hit women. Anyway, killing them was different, killing was business, nothing personal, and he killed cleanly. He was not into torture or anything of that kind.

He'd followed the man, who had made his job even easier by going off-piste to ski. It had been a beautiful morning. Luckily no-one was around as they were obeying the danger signs that were posted along the run. He prided himself on being an excellent skier, so once his target took off from the top of the slope, he seized the opportunity and followed him.

He saw the edge of the ravine coming up, and before the man got the chance to turn, he nudged him, sending him flying over the edge. Stopping momentarily to check, he knew his target would not survive the fall.

He had enjoyed the rest of the holiday while being paid a handsome sum for the job.

If only similar luck were with him on this trip. He had hoped for a repeat and looked forward to enjoying the cruise, but it wasn't to be. Not every job was easy, but he had planned this one in great detail, and the woman should have died in Lisbon. Instead, she was very much alive and inadvertently dodging his every move.

He was determined not to fail this time.

# Chapter 22

Rachel felt truly happy for the first time in weeks, pleased that she and Carlos could be friends without the pressure of anything more. She was sure that she could control her feelings for him with only three days and four nights of cruising left. Adding the finishing touches to her makeup, she made her way down to deck four for dinner.

Carlos was waiting for her outside the dining room and he flashed one of his most disarming smiles at her. She felt her heart miss a beat at the sight of him and took a deep breath before taking the arm he offered her.

*Yep, really under control!*

Dinner was enjoyable as always, and Rachel noticed that Marjorie was seated at her usual table with an elderly man. She seemed happy, and they were engrossed in conversation. Rachel smiled at her and Marjorie waved.

After dinner, Rachel and Carlos were the last to leave the table as usual. Marjorie was enjoying something that looked like a coffee liqueur, and Rachel was floating on air that all was well again with her world.

"Where to this evening, ma'am?" Carlos joked.

"Let's go and listen to the string quartet in the atrium, shall we?"

"Your wish is my command."

They left together, Rachel remembering that she had one more thing she needed to do before she completely forgot about the Marjorie thing.

She turned to Carlos. "Will you find us some seats? I just need to go and get a shawl from my room so that we can enjoy a walk outside later."

For once, Rachel took the lift up to deck nine and made her way along the corridor. Relieved to see that Josie was back on stateroom duties, she headed towards her.

"Good evening, ma'am Rachel," said Josie, smiling.

"Good evening, Josie. Is your hand alright? I understand you burnt it." Rachel looked at the neatly bandaged hand.

"Yes, ma'am. It's feeling much better. The Doctor fixed it up nicely for me and the nurses will be changing the dressings each day to stop it getting infected."

Rachel wasn't quite sure how to broach the subject. "Did you finish early last night?"

"No, ma'am, I always finish my work." She looked alarmed as if she might get into trouble.

"Of course you do. I wouldn't have thought otherwise. I saw Daniel last night, though, working along our corridor and leaving my room," she lied. "It is normally you I see, so I was a bit worried about whether you had been seriously hurt."

"No, ma'am Rachel, I got waylaid with one of the guests who was having trouble sleeping and I had to go to housekeeping to get new pillows for him, so Daniel finished the last few rooms down your end. Housekeeping don't like the assistants going down there for items."

"I see," said Rachel thoughtfully. "So you didn't do Lady Snellthorpe's room last night?"

"No, ma'am." Josie was looking more concerned. "There wasn't a problem with the room, was there, ma'am Rachel? No-one said."

"Oh no, Josie, nothing like that. I missed you that's all. I'm really pleased to see you back. Goodnight."

"Goodnight, ma'am Rachel."

Rachel went into her room and struggled to breathe. She hadn't been imagining things after all, and if Josie was to be believed, it had not been her in Marjorie's room. The cobwebs fell away from her brain and she sprang into police mode.

*Marjorie is in danger. I need to find her.*

She changed into comfortable shoes and then marched rapidly along the corridor, almost knocking a tray out of Daniel's hands.

"Sorry," she muttered, but didn't stop. She ran down the stairs towards the restaurant, forgetting all about Carlos, and walked straight through to Marjorie's table.

Second sitting dining had begun and there was a young couple seated at the table.

Stavros turned towards her. "Did you forget something, ma'am?"

"No, Stavros, I wanted to ask Lady Snellthorpe something. Do you know where she went?"

"No, ma'am. Sorry."

"I heard her saying she was going for a breath of air." Geraldine had been taking orders nearby and obviously overheard the conversation.

"Thank you, Geraldine." Rachel turned so quickly she just missed Grigor, the wine waiter, who was bringing wine to the young couple at Marjorie's table. "I'm so sorry," she spluttered and marched out of the restaurant at break-neck speed. A sense of urgency was building up in her. Although she was aware of the looks she was getting as she half-barged past people in her hurry to get out, she didn't care.

She opted for the lift, deciding to start on deck fourteen and work her way up from there. There were queues of people waiting for the lifts and she could feel her heart pounding in her chest as the frustration built. In spite of there being six lifts, they were all full with people going out for evening entertainment. Finally one stopped that she could get into, but just as she was pressing the 'close doors' button, someone else pressed the 'open doors' one. She glared at the man who was holding the lift open, obviously waiting for someone.

The man's companion eventually arrived, but then the lift stopped at every floor on the way up to deck fourteen. Rachel was beginning to curse herself for not taking the stairs, but she had a full stomach and it would have been counter-productive.

At last, the lift stopped at the right deck. Rachel decided to take a clockwise walk from her starting point, searching around the deck. She walked more slowly now, not wanting to miss Marjorie, and she noticed that the deck was eerily quiet. Most people were eating or enjoying shows, and apart from the bow where the outdoor cinema screen was, there were not many people around.

Having circled the front of the ship, she was heading to the rear when she thought she heard footsteps behind her. Looking round anxiously, she saw a drunken man making his way towards one of the doors leading inside. Rachel continued walking, and now all she could hear was the sound of distant music and the ship forcing its way through the waves.

The tension was building in her head and in her temples, and she was beginning to feel the night-time chill as she hadn't put on a shawl or jacket. Goose bumps were building on her shoulders as she turned the corner at the back of the ship.

Suddenly, she heard a scream and turned to see a body hurtling down the stairs towards her. She managed to run up the stairs just in time to catch the woman in her arms, and they both fell backwards. Rachel felt a searing pain as her left foot caught underneath one of the steps as she fell.

It took a while for her to get her breath back, but she knew immediately it was Marjorie lying on top of her, moaning.

"Marjorie! Are you alright?" Rachel managed to move slightly and shift the weight.

"I think so." Rachel was so relieved to hear her voice. "Thanks to you."

At that moment, a couple arrived as a good-looking man came down the stairs in a black dinner suit. His manner was reassuring, and he sent the couple away to find a crew member.

"What happened? Are you both alright? Does anything hurt?" His deep Italian voice filled the evening air. As Rachel was starting to feel agonising pain in her left ankle, everything looked a little hazy, so she tried to focus on the man's eyes. He looked away and glanced around, as if unsure what to do next, but he didn't need to decide as an officer appeared on the scene.

"Medical team are on the way, don't move, ladies."

Rachel just managed to ask the officer to look after Marjorie, who was now shaking, before she passed out.

# Chapter 23

Sarah was on call, catching up with paperwork in the medical centre, when the emergency bleep went off.

"Two passengers injured deck fourteen, stern."

She called Brigitte to join her with the stretcher.

"Can you track down Dr Bentley and ask him to join us?" she asked reception, putting the phone down. On her way out of the medical centre, she saw that Alex was still there.

"Accident, deck fourteen. We might need you," she said as she pulled the hefty emergency bag along behind her. He finished whatever he was drinking from a mug and followed her. Brigitte ran in, and seeing that Alex was already carrying the stretcher, she followed them.

The medical centre was midships on deck two, so it was a long way to race up to deck fourteen. They took the crew lift and then ran along the deck to where they had been told the incident had occurred.

Sarah was shocked and horrified to see Rachel and Lady Snellthorpe lying on the floor. A small crowd had gathered around. "Clear the scene, please," she instructed the officer. "But keep hold of witnesses. Rachel!" Sarah called her name. "Rachel!"

The officer explained that Rachel had fainted shortly after he'd arrived, then she had come to, only to pass out again.

Rachel opened her eyes and tried to smile. "Marjorie?"

"She's okay, Doctor Romano is seeing to her. What happened?"

"Not sure, Marjorie fell, caught, landed…"

She passed out again.

Graham arrived and took over the assessment of Rachel's injuries.

"Did anyone see what happened?" Sarah asked the officer.

"No, but this gentleman was on the scene when I arrived." He turned to his right, but there was a no-one there. "Sorry, looks like he's gone. He was dressed in a tux so may have been on his way out. He did tell me that he arrived after another couple and they didn't see what happened, either."

Graham carried out his examination.

"Left ankle is badly swollen, probably broken. Right arm is cut up – she'll need a bit of glue, but I think she managed to land without hitting her head. No lumps or contusions." He proceeded to feel each vertebra along Rachel's spine, assessing for pain and asking Rachel if it hurt. Rachel was mumbling negatives. "Let's get her to the infirmary and do a full head injury assessment there. Try to wake her up, Sarah, and keep her awake. Put her in a collar and use the spinal stretcher until I have assessed her properly. Right, team, let's get on with it."

Bernard arrived with a spinal stretcher, and after applying a neck collar for support, he and Sarah moved Rachel onto this. Sarah knew that Graham needed to rule out spinal fractures, but according to the officer who had attended the scene, Rachel had been moving all of her limbs around before passing out.

Alex and Brigitte had already left with Lady Snellthorpe on the first stretcher. Sarah was concerned for Rachel and held her hand, speaking to her all the way to the infirmary and exchanging worried glances with Graham. Sarah knew they were both thinking the same thing: it looked very much like Rachel had been right all along and that there really was a threat to Marjorie's life. It was hard to believe that anyone would want to harm this sweet old lady, but obviously, someone did.

Before he left, Graham asked the officers to get the names of everyone present and find out if anyone had seen anything.

"I want to see security later, but for now, I need to make sure these passengers are assessed properly."

Once they were in the infirmary, he made a full assessment of both patients. Lady Snellthorpe had a few bruises to her right arm and chest, but other than being severely shaken, she was not seriously hurt.

X-rays of Rachel's back, ankle and knee were taken, and it was established there were no spinal fractures. The X-ray confirmed her ankle was broken, but it was a simple fracture. Rachel had become more alert, but was clearly still in pain. Lady Snellthorpe was in the bed next to her, looking concerned.

"Are you alright, my dear? I was so worried about you."

Rachel tried to smile, but Bernard was shining a torch in her eyes and she flinched instead.

"Apart from feeling like I've been in a boxing ring, I feel fine."

"You've got a broken ankle," Sarah explained. "We can't give you any painkillers until we're sure you haven't got a head injury. Can you remember what happened?"

"I had found out that the person I heard in Marjorie's room last night wasn't Josie, and so I went in search of her, fearing the worst." Rachel looked apologetically at Lady Snellthorpe, but continued, "I went to the dining room and one of the waiters said that she had headed out for air, so I started my search on deck fourteen. I searched from midships port side and went in a clockwise direction. When I got to turn to the stairs on starboard, rear, I heard movement. That's when I saw Marjorie and I just reacted by running up a few steps and catching her as she fell. I think I caught my left foot under the step as I fell and I landed on my right side. I didn't bang my head, and most of the fall was broken by

191

my right hand and elbow. I think catching my foot helped me to support Marjorie."

"Did you see anyone else?" asked Graham.

"I saw a shadow at the top of the steps, but it was too quick. After I fell, a couple arrived, and then a good-looking man in a tuxedo appeared and helped. He may have seen who it was at the top of the steps."

Rachel tried to get up.

"Stay still, Rachel," said Sarah. "You're not going anywhere."

"No, young lady. Bernard is going to put you into a back slab, and then you'll need to go the hospital in Gibraltar tomorrow to see the orthopaedic surgeon who will probably put you in a walking plaster as the break seems to be a simple one. Now we know you didn't bang your head, you are going to have a pain killing injection and get some sleep."

Rachel turned to Lady Snellthorpe. "What do you remember?"

"I remember walking along the outside of deck fifteen, enjoying the evening air. Ralph and I always took a walk after dinner, so it's force of habit. I was looking at the stars and I could hear the waves crashing against the ship's side, as if they were objecting to this monstrous beast daring to break their rhythm, when I felt there was someone there. I turned to see and felt a shove in my back, and the next thing, I felt myself falling. Then I saw you were there, Rachel, catching me. As I lay on top of you, I thought you were dead and I went into shock, but then you spoke to me. You saved my life, dear."

Graham explained that he had called security and would explain to them what had happened, but he didn't want either Lady Snellthorpe or Rachel to be interviewed until the morning.

"You both need a good night's sleep. Bernard, please give a sedative to Lady Snellthorpe and pethidine injection to Rachel. Sarah will stay with you and a member of security will be outside the door."

He smiled at them both.

Sarah was pleased to be left alone with Rachel and Lady Snellthorpe. Bernard had given Rachel an injection, and she was already looking quite woozy while he was putting on the back slab plaster.

"What is a back slab, anyway?" she asked.

"It's a slab of plaster, left open at the front, that will support the break while allowing the limb to swell up underneath. Once the swelling is down, a proper plaster can be applied."

"Sorry about the apes." Rachel turned to Sarah.

"You did warn me you didn't want to see them, but I didn't realise you would go to this much trouble to avoid them," Sarah replied. "I am just pleased that you and Lady Snellthorpe are not seriously injured."

Rachel smirked at her friend.

"I'd hate to know what you consider a serious injury."

# Chapter 24

The next morning, Rachel woke up feeling like she had been mauled. It took her a while to register where she was, but soon the events of the previous evening came to mind.

She managed to sit herself up in the infirmary bed. Her left ankle felt sore but supported, and she noticed the cuts to her right arm had been dressed. Her ribs felt tender where Marjorie had landed on her right side. Sarah was asleep in a chair at the side of her bed and Marjorie was lying awake in the bed to her right, looking shaken.

"Good morning." Rachel smiled at the old lady.

"Good morning, my dear." Marjorie sounded as low as she looked. Rachel noticed a tear falling down her face. "I'm so sorry you have been injured because of me."

"It's not you who should be sorry," said Rachel. "It's the person who tried to—"

Rachel stopped, seeing that the realisation that someone was trying to kill her was sinking into Marjorie's mind.

"Why?" she asked. "I'm just a doddery old lady who will be dead in a few years anyway."

"Perhaps whoever is doing this can't wait a few years." Rachel spoke quietly. "Do you have any idea who that could be?"

"The idea doesn't bear thinking about. I just can't believe it."

Sarah woke up at that moment and heard the last part of the conversation. "I hope you two slept well," she said.

"Hi," said Rachel. "That knock-out injection definitely helped, but I feel pretty sore now."

"I'll get you some pain killers and anti-inflammatories. We are docked in Gibraltar so will need to head to the hospital soon. Dr Bentley has phoned ahead."

Sarah left the infirmary and returned with four tablets and fresh water. She also handed Marjorie some tablets to take. Marjorie looked unsure.

"A sedative, and your blood-pressure pills. Do you have any pain?"

"No, dear, only pain in the heart, and I don't think there are any tablets for that," she said, looking away.

Rachel understood how difficult this must be for Marjorie and she could see that Sarah sensed it too. There was not much they could say to help, but they tried to keep Marjorie in the present with light conversation.

Dr Bentley came into the room accompanied by a smartly dressed man with the customary three gold stripes on his epaulettes, signifying his status as a senior officer. The man had short greying hair and stood tall at around six feet, Rachel estimated, and his uniform was tight, implying some recent weight gain.

"Glad to see you two looking better than last night." Dr Bentley smiled. "This is Chief Security Officer Waverley and he would like to ask you some questions. I have filled him in on your previous concerns, Rachel, but he will want to know more about all of the events. Are you feeling up to it?"

Rachel nodded and Marjorie remained quiet but attentive. CSO Waverley took a seat in between the beds and started by turning towards Marjorie.

"Lady Snellthorpe, firstly may I say how sorry I and the captain are that you have been attacked on board the *Coral Queen*. We take this sort of thing very seriously, and I will do everything within my power to find out who is responsible for this. I'll be reporting directly to the captain on the matter." He paused for a moment as if to allow the enormity of his words to sink in. "Please start from the beginning. Have you noticed anything out of the ordinary since the start of your cruise?"

Marjorie sighed a deep sigh.

"If only Ralph were here, he would know what to do," she said quietly, but then she straightened up and continued. "The only things I have noticed have been feelings which seemed silly at the time, but may or may not be important."

"Go on," Waverley encouraged.

"Well, I kept feeling I was being watched, but it didn't make any sense. I put it down to travelling alone for the first time since Ralph's death." She paused for a moment and Rachel could see she was trying hard to remain in control. "There was a man I recognised, but I can't remember where from, and that has concerned me all through the cruise."

"Who is this man?" The CSO leaned forward, taking notes.

"It's a man who sits at Rachel's dinner table and he seems to have become a friend." Marjorie looked apologetically at Rachel. "It is probably nothing. We met so many people through Ralph's work and his charities."

Rachel felt herself redden and her heart was beating rapidly. All eyes had now turned towards her.

"Do you know who Lady Snellthorpe is referring to?" asked Waverley.

"I think she means Carlos," Rachel answered softly.

"Please can you tell us about Carlos?"

"To be honest, I don't know very much about him at all. We met through the dining arrangements and have become friends, but I don't even know his last name." Rachel was starting to feel like a complete idiot and looked to Sarah for support. Sarah nodded encouragement.

"What does he do? Where is he from?"

"I've just remembered, I was supposed to meet him in the atrium last night, but I returned to my room to ask Josie about the noise I heard in Marjorie's room the night before. When Josie said it wasn't her, I forgot all about him and went in search of Marjorie. He never told me what he did. I tried to ask, but he said that he wanted to forget about work for a few weeks. I was feeling the same way, so I understood where he was coming from in that respect. He lives in London that's all I know."

Rachel wanted to tell them about her suspicions regarding Carlos, but she couldn't bring herself to do so. Not until she had challenged him herself.

"What table number do you dine at?" Waverley asked.

"Table 305," Rachel replied sadly. She felt Sarah squeeze her hand as the CSO turned his attention back to Marjorie, but not before jotting the table number down in his notebook.

"Please continue, Lady Snellthorpe."

Lady Snellthorpe glanced at Rachel before going on.

"The next thing was the accident in Lisbon."

Rachel noticed the CSO shuffle in his seat, looking a bit embarrassed as Marjorie related the events of the accident that had taken the life of Freda McDonald. "She was wearing my coat and hat, you see, and when I looked at her in the road afterwards, I was shocked by how much it looked like me lying there. I was shaken to the core, but as it seemed to be a tragic accident, I put it to the back of my mind. I was also very ill afterwards so wasn't quite myself."

The CSO turned to Dr Bentley at this stage in the story. "We were alerted by the Portuguese police that a boy may or may not have witnessed someone pushing the lady into the road."

Marjorie let out a gasp at this point, looking shocked.

"I'm sorry, Lady Snellthorpe," said Dr Bentley. "It was my decision not to alarm you with that information because the boy's story could not be verified, and the coroner delivered an accidental death verdict a few days later. Security were aware, though, and kept a close eye on you."

Marjorie looked angry, but said nothing.

Waverley continued. "We had plain clothes security officers following you for a few days until the Portuguese police closed the case."

"I see," said Marjorie, clearly exasperated. "Once I began to feel well again, I carried on with the cruise as Ralph would have wanted me to, and I didn't notice anything else – other than the feeling of being followed, which could have been your men." She looked scathingly at CSO Waverley at this point. "Until last night, when I was definitely pushed. Had it not been for Rachel, I would not have been here to tell the story, and it would have appeared to be another accidental death."

Waverley coughed and turned to Rachel. "What about you, Miss Prince? Or should I say WPC Prince? Where do you come in?"

Rachel noticed that Marjorie looked surprised again at the mention of her being a policewoman.

"This is going to sound like I read too many novels, but I first noticed Marjorie before we boarded. I was in the departure lounge and I saw her enter through the VIP entrance. I couldn't help noticing how concerned her chauffeur looked as he left her and I thought it was odd."

It was Rachel's turn to look apologetically at Marjorie.

"Chance put us into rooms next door to each other and we became friends. I, too, had the feeling of being watched, and I had a gut feeling that Marjorie was in danger, but I couldn't see any reason for this. I have been working flat out to get through my PC assessments and thrown myself into work for several months, so I put it all down to an overactive imagination and stress."

Choosing not to mention Robert, Rachel went on to explain about the night of the drunk in the corridor outside Marjorie's room and how he had been sent away by another guest. She reiterated the concerns she'd had after Freda's death in Lisbon, which to all intents and purposes had been put down to a tragic accident, and then she went on to explain about the night she had returned to her room and heard noises in the room next door. She missed out any suspicions she'd had regarding Carlos.

"You must have thought I was mad, snatching the tablets away from your bedside table."

"I did wonder what that was all about," agreed Marjorie.

"Anyway, the tablets were examined by Dr Bentley and they were the ones he had prescribed, so I assumed that it had been Josie, the stateroom attendant, who had been in your room."

Dr Bentley looked embarrassed as Rachel recalled their conversation and how he had reassured her that her suspicions were all in her mind.

"I couldn't put it to rest completely until I had spoken to Josie. Sorry, Doctor. I went back to my stateroom last night and asked her about it, and she confirmed that she had not been anywhere near your room that night, Marjorie, because she had to collect pillows for another guest and she got behind on her work. At that point, I was really worried and went searching for you. The rest is history."

"Thank heavens you did," said Marjorie, and the others nodded agreement.

"Do you remember anything else from last night? Did you see who pushed Lady Snellthorpe?" asked Waverley.

"No. I have racked my brains, and all I saw was a shadow. I reacted on impulse to catch Marjorie before she landed. There was a man who came downstairs and helped us though. He may have seen something."

Waverley coughed again. "We can't seem to find him. The officer attending had asked him to wait around, but in the melee he seems to have disappeared. We think he was probably on his way out, and once help was at hand, he left."

Rachel explained how he had seemed distracted. "I was ready to pass out, but I remember he was looking around as if weighing up what to do next when the officer appeared on the scene. I don't remember much after that."

"I guess he was looking for help," said Dr Bentley. "He was probably worried about you both."

"I realise you have to go to the hospital any minute," said the CSO, "but we would like to get a detailed description of this man from you later so that we can try and trace him."

He turned back to Marjorie.

"There is no easy way to ask this, Lady Snellthorpe, but do you know anyone who would want you dead?"

Lady Snellthorpe looked thoughtful. "In all honesty, Officer Waverley. No, but if you want to know who would benefit the most from my death, it would be my son, Jeremy."

"I think I have taken up enough of your time." CSO Waverley got up to leave. "I will see you again later, Miss Prince."

Rachel nodded, but she was more concerned about Marjorie. How would the old lady cope if her son were arrested for attempting to murder her?

# Chapter 25

Sarah pushed Rachel's wheelchair through security and off the ship. A taxi was waiting to take them to the clinic, and Sarah held the X-rays taken the previous night. The clinic was just a few minutes' drive away, and they were seated in the waiting room within ten minutes of leaving the cruise terminal.

A doctor called them through into a clinic room, and after examining the X-rays and Rachel's ankle, he agreed it was a simple fracture of the fibula bone at the base of the ankle. He had introduced himself as Mr Ram, and after mumbling for a little while, he turned his attention to Rachel.

"We can get you put into a lightweight walking plaster, but you will not be able to walk on it until the plaster is dry. Your cast will be fibreglass and it usually hardens within an hour, but I would suggest you don't walk on it until tonight. You will still need to support yourself with crutches to prevent you putting too much weight onto the ankle. I will prescribe some painkillers and anti-inflammatory tablets to reduce the swelling. You should go to your local fracture clinic when you return home and show them the X-rays. Chances are you will be in the plaster boot for six weeks, and then it will be another six weeks of physiotherapy until you feel normal again. What do you do for a living?"

"I'm a policewoman," Rachel replied.

"Ah, you will be confined to desk duties until your ankle is healed, I suspect, but you can go to work. Nurse! Fibreglass plastic boot, please, and crutches."

"A man of few words," said Sarah as Rachel was wheeled into the plaster room.

A tall nurse with light brown hair tied up in a bun which reminded Rachel of missionary nurses, came into the plaster room, wearing blue scrubs similar to those which Sarah wore when she was in the medical centre.

"Miss Prince?"

"Yes," answered Rachel.

"Hi, I'm Chloe. I'm going to apply your new plaster. Have you had painkillers recently?"
Rachel nodded.

"All I need to know then is what colour plaster you would like." Chloe brought out a trolley with an array of different colour packages.

"I had no idea there were so many different colours," Rachel said. "I'm tempted by the pink, but it might clash with my red dress. I think I'll just go for the plain beige one, please. It will go better with my other leg."

Chloe was very efficient at removing the back slab and applying the new plaster, and the whole procedure was over in fifteen minutes. After this, Chloe gave Rachel an instruction sheet on how to look after the plaster and prevent a deep vein thrombosis from occurring.

"By the way," Chloe called out as Rachel was leaving, "don't be fooled by how light that plaster is. It sets like rock, so don't go kicking anybody."

"I'll bear that in mind," Rachel replied, cackling.
As they were leaving the hospital, Sarah asked. "How do you feel?"

"A lot better after taking more painkillers, thanks. If you don't mind wheeling me around, I'm happy to go somewhere."

"I'm game! Let's go into town. It's a fairly flat walk, and even with the heat, it will be nice." The temperature was climbing as it got closer to midday, but it was a pleasant, dry heat rather than a humid heat, so Rachel agreed.

Town was busy with cruise ship passengers, and it all seemed rather familiar. Gibraltar was British, and it showed. The signs were in English and Rachel could hear English being spoken all around her.

They passed through a large archway into a big courtyard area with lots of cafés and outdoor seating. Sarah chose a spot in the shade and sat down. Pulling a chair towards Rachel, she ordered her to elevate her leg while they rested.

A waiter was soon with them and they ordered ice cold colas. "Anything to eat?" the waiter asked.

"You know what?" said Rachel. "I'm starving; I haven't eaten since last night." She chose fish and chips from the menu, and Sarah opted for steak and chips.

"The one thing I miss more than anything else is British chips," Sarah remarked. "I love foreign food, but you can't beat good old traditional chips."

Rachel agreed and found herself looking forward to getting back to Leeds after the trip was over although she still had the matter of Carlos to resolve.

"Work is going to love me!" she laughed. "I go on a cruise and come home with a broken ankle. By the way that doctor didn't ask for my medical insurance documents."

"Don't worry about that. The cruise line is paying for all your treatment, and Marjorie's. I reckon you will also be in line for some compensation."

Rachel smiled. "Now that's the best thing I've heard all day, but I hadn't even thought about it."

"They can afford it. I have known them reach five or six figure payout agreements rather than having an insurance claim brought against them. The cruise lines take the safety of their passengers very seriously, and its reputation even more seriously. The last thing they want is a bad headline. They are none too happy that there is a murderer loose on their ship I can tell you."

"I don't doubt it, I can't say I'm very happy about it, either. I wonder if it is the son that is behind this. It seems a very callous thing to do."

"It is an awful thing to think, isn't it? Poor Marjorie, she must be at her wits' end."

"I just hope the stress doesn't finish her off. I have grown so fond of her and would hate anything to happen to her."

"I know what you mean; she is very likeable, and whoever is behind this is a heartless psychopath. Speaking of fondness – what about Carlos? Do you think he's involved?"

"I sincerely hope not, but I can't be sure. At times, he does behave suspiciously, and I've had my doubts since the accident in Lisbon. I thought I saw him running away from the scene there, but he said he was nowhere near that area."

Sarah looked shocked. "You never said!"

"Everything seemed to settle down afterwards, and I was never one hundred percent certain it was him. I would hate to accuse someone wrongly, but now that Marjorie says she recognises him from somewhere, I am left with huge doubts. The thing is, we have become close, and I was hoping something would develop."

Rachel could see the sympathy in Sarah's eyes as she took a long drink of cola. "Maybe he's not involved at all," Sarah said. "Remember there's that other man you saw last night, too. Perhaps he saw something, or perhaps he is involved."

Rachel knew that CSO Waverley would be checking Carlos out even while they were seated in the café. It wouldn't be too hard to track him down from the seating plans.

"We will know soon enough, I guess. Do you think I will ever find the right man? It seems I'm destined to pick the wrong ones. It's hard to believe that six months ago, my whole future was mapped out, and now I'm like a ship without a rudder – to use a nautical expression."

At that moment, their meals arrived and they tucked in hungrily. Sarah spoke first.

"I think you will definitely find a good man. You and I have both had our man troubles, but there's still plenty of time, and to use another nautical expression – there are plenty more fish in the sea."

Rachel enjoyed the time with Sarah and, as always, felt much more normal in the presence of her friend. She wished they still shared a flat together; life would be so much easier with Sarah around.

*Perhaps I can buy my own flat if the compensation is as good as Sarah suggests it will be.*

After lunch, Sarah pushed Rachel up the main High Street which was packed with people and shops. As a tax haven, with no VAT added to goods, Gibraltar proved to be very attractive to cruise tourists with lots of money to spend. Neither Rachel nor Sarah were in the mood for extravagant spending although Rachel did buy her mum a pair of gold earrings and her dad a new camera case. Sarah topped up on toiletries and then offered to take Rachel back to the ship.

"You should get that leg elevated now to keep the swelling down," she said, and Rachel laughed.

"Okay, Nurse Bradshaw!"

They caught one of the regular buses that ferried cruise passengers to and from the terminal. Sarah folded the lightweight wheelchair and placed it in the aisle while Rachel manoeuvred her way on with the aid of crutches. Rachel was happy to get back to the ship and asked Sarah to take her straight to her room so that she could get some rest before facing the CSO again. She was dreading going to dinner, and she was particularly dreading what news there might be on Carlos.

Once in her room, she climbed onto the bed, took some painkillers and went to sleep.

# Chapter 26

Rachel awoke to banging on the stateroom door. It took a moment for her to realise where she was as she still felt groggy. As she went to move, she felt the plaster on her leg and pain in her ankle, which reminded her of what had happened.

She hobbled to the door as she hadn't quite mastered the walking plaster technique yet. Looking through the spy hole, she saw Sarah and opened the door.

Her friend came bustling in. "I was so worried about you. I phoned three times, and you didn't answer, and I've been banging on the door for ages. I was just about to call Josie to open up."

"Sorry, I was out for the count. I think these painkillers are taking their toll. What time is it?" Her room was dark because she had closed the curtains before climbing into bed.

"It's eight o'clock. We set sail an hour ago and I think you may have missed your dinner."

"That's perhaps as well, I don't want to run into Carlos. I'll get something at the buffet. Are you joining me?"

"Yes, I will. I'll just give Waverley a ring and tell him we'll be along in an hour. Is that alright with you?"

Rachel sighed. "Yes, I guess we have to get it over with. Sarah, I really need to wash. How am I supposed to shower with this plaster in place?"

"Da-daaa!" Sarah opened a package she had been holding and held up a long plastic boot with a rubber seal at the opening. "Meet your shower helper. I'll show you how to put it on, and then you can do it for yourself after today."

Sarah helped Rachel pull the boot over her plaster and showed her how it secured itself against her leg, allowing her to get into a shower or bath without wetting the plaster.

"You're the best!" exclaimed Rachel.

"More good news to come. The captain has secured two luxury suites for you and Lady Snellthorpe to stay in for the rest of the cruise. They have large bathrooms and are on deck fifteen. You will have a butler and can order anything you like, on the house. Josie will pack up your room, and your belongings will be moved for you." Sarah was oozing excitement now.

"Okay, so what's the bad news?"

"You will have a security guard stationed outside your rooms for the rest of the cruise, and Marjorie will be escorted everywhere. From a discreet distance, of course."

Rachel groaned and went for a shower. It was a lot more difficult than she'd thought it would be, showering with her leg in plaster. Even with the plastic boot, she felt clumsy and awkward. They were later than they thought they'd be going up to the buffet for dinner, so Sarah let CSO Waverley know that they had been held up.

Rachel was glad of the crutches as she still felt unsteady walking on the plaster cast, but she knew she would master it soon enough. *Three more nights to go.* She was pleased that she would soon be home, having called her parents from Gibraltar. They had agreed to collect her from Southampton so that she wouldn't have to negotiate luggage and train travel with a broken ankle. She hadn't been completely honest with them about how she sustained her injuries, deciding to fill them in on the real story when she got back. For now, they just knew she had fallen down some steps and broken her ankle.

Sarah insisted Rachel sit down when they got to the buffet, and then she went and got food for her, returning a second time for her own food. *It is good to have Sarah around*, thought Rachel. They enjoyed their food, and the waiters, who normally didn't serve from the buffet, kept coming over to offer them more food or drinks.

After she had eaten, Rachel felt a bit more like herself, albeit a slightly light-headed self.

"How's Marjorie?" she asked.

"Still a bit shaken, but she has already been moved to her suite and is being waited on hand and foot by the butler you will share. I think it will be difficult for her until she finds out what and who is behind all of this although I think we all know the *who*!"

"Does her son know he is under suspicion?"

"I'm not sure. Waverley is going to fill us in on the investigation once we see him, and he wants to talk to you some more, so I suppose we should get on with it." Sarah smiled sympathetically. They got up to leave, but as they did so, Rachel spotted someone out of the corner of her eye.

"That's him! That's the man from last night."

"Where?" By the time Sarah had turned to look, the man had gone, and Rachel was not capable of going after him. "Did he see you?"

"I don't think so, he was looking the opposite way. If only he had come forward so that we could eliminate him from our enquiries."

"Now you are sounding like a police constable," said Sarah, laughing. "Come on, PC Plod, let's plod along to your new suite. Waverley will meet us there."

Rachel picked up her crutches and walked slowly towards the lifts. On arrival at deck fifteen, Sarah led the way to the starboard side, but this time they were heading towards the stern of the ship. The suite was at the very back in the corner, and Sarah pointed to another one in the opposite corner on the port side.

"That's Marjorie's room."

Rachel was pleased to arrive, and on entering the room, she let out a whoop. It was about four times the size of her balcony suite, and there was a separate seating area and a huge bathroom with a tub as well as a shower. She walked through to the lounge area and saw a large flat screen TV hanging on the wall, a settee which was also a bed, a computer on a desk and a huge fridge.

"Was this not in use?" she asked Sarah.

"Apparently both suites were vacated in Gibraltar as the family were heading over to an apartment they own in Spain before flying home."

"It's wonderful," said Rachel as she opened the fridge and found it fully stocked. There were flowers on the table and a fruit bowl filled with exotic fruits.

There was a knock at the door and Sarah went to answer it. CSO Waverley entered, smiling. It was the first time Rachel had seen him smile. That morning he had been very serious and his whole demeanour had reflected the gravity of the situation, but now he appeared a little more relaxed.

*Perhaps because no more murders have taken place.*

"I trust your new accommodation suits?" he said.

"Yes, I think it will do, thank you." Rachel noticed a tall, skinny man standing alongside Waverley, who he now turned to.

"This is Security Officer Ravanos. He will be guarding you and Lady Snellthorpe for the rest of the

215

journey. He will be relieved at night by Security Officer McColgan."

Rachel was about to ask whether this was all necessary, but decided against it as she didn't want to cause any problems. On reflection, she was pleased that Marjorie would be protected.

"How will he guard both of us?" she asked instead.

"Well, Lady Snellthorpe will be his priority because we don't really think that you are in any danger. It is unlikely the killer knows who you are, but if you could let your guard know where you are going at all times, that would be helpful."

"How is the investigation going?" asked Sarah.

CSO Waverley pointed to a seat. "Do you mind if I sit down?" Rachel nodded towards the chair and Waverley sat. "I'm afraid we don't have any leads on the potential killer yet, but head office is going through the passenger manifest with a fine toothcomb and anyone with a criminal record will be brought to my attention by the morning. The police in London have been informed and they will start investigating the Snellthorpe family and business connections to see what that brings up. I have asked them not to alert Jeremy Snellthorpe, just in case he is involved, so their enquiries will be discreet. At present we have no real leads, and the man who assisted you last evening has not come forward. We did put out a request over the ship-wide speaker during the day and will do so again tomorrow morning, in case he was off ship. We could do with a description from you, though, if that is possible?"

He paused for a moment.

"We have managed to find out more about your—" He coughed. "Your *acquaintance*, Carlos."

Rachel stiffened and sat up; he had her full attention. She had been dreading whatever it was she was about to hear.

"It turns out his full name is Carlos Jacobi. He is a Private Detective who was hired to keep an eye on Lady Snellthorpe and make sure she was kept safe. He hasn't been very good at his job by all accounts, but we can confirm that he is who he says he is, and that he is not under suspicion."

Rachel had stopped breathing, but she now felt huge relief mixed with anger. Carlos was not a murderer, but she was angry with herself as much as with him because she had obviously distracted him from his job.

"Who hired him?"

"He won't say. Says his clients are confidential and he won't budge on it. I think he probably doesn't want us telling his employer what a mess he's made of his job, to be honest. We have checked his ID, though, and his firm has done work for the Snellthorpe family in the past – mainly for the former Lord Snellthorpe."

"That's why Marjorie thought she recognised him," said Rachel. "Has he discovered anything while on board?"

"He says he thought he saw someone running away from the scene in Lisbon and gave chase, but lost sight of the man as he was prevented from getting far by the crowds. He then returned to the scene and saw you getting into a taxi with Lady Snellthorpe, so he knew she was safe. He continued following her, but spotted our men following, too, so he assumed she would be under permanent surveillance and relaxed his guard. As did we, unfortunately."

"I see," said Rachel. She now knew that she had seen Carlos running away in Lisbon, but not for the reasons she had feared. CSO Waverley's words also clarified why Marjorie had felt she was being followed.

"All in all, it's a bit of a mess. Our security team made themselves too obvious." Waverley glared at SO Ravanos, who appeared to squirm a little, and then looked back to Rachel. "Mr Jacobi was unable to give a description of the man he chased, other than he was about six feet tall with dark hair, and that description fits about five hundred passengers. I don't think the killer will try again though. He may think he succeeded with his last attempt."

*I doubt that,* thought Rachel.

"Surely he would have stayed around to check – unless the other passengers scared him off." Sarah echoed the same concern. "Wouldn't he have kept watch to make sure she was dead?"

"Well, if he did, he will know he wasn't successful," answered Waverley, looking uncomfortable. "I still think he will give up. He has made two unsuccessful attempts on Lady Snellthorpe's life, possibly three if we count the probability of it being he who was in her stateroom the other night. He will know that we are onto him now so he would be mad to try again. Nevertheless, we are not taking any chances, and Lady Snellthorpe will be guarded at all times. However, I think this crime will now only be solved by the British police, unless our passenger checks come up with someone of interest."

"What about Marjorie's friend?" asked Rachel.

"The police in Scotland have been informed, and they have broken it to the family that the death is now being treated as suspicious and a case of mistaken identity. That's all we can say for now, unless we can find out more. Now, Miss Prince, perhaps you could give us a description of the man who assisted you last night."

Rachel gave as full a description as she could, explaining that she thought she had seen the man leaving the buffet this evening, and with that Waverley left. Ravanos was posted in the corridor with both staterooms in sight. Sarah stayed for a while and then hugged her friend goodnight after making sure Rachel was going to be alright.

"Goodnight, Rachel. Sleep tight."

"I think I will with all of these tablets." Rachel laughed as she locked her door and looked at the time –

half past midnight. She took her pills and went to bed, admiring the opulence of the room she was now in.

Carlos's face appeared before her as she drifted off. At least she didn't have to worry about him being involved any more, but she couldn't help but wonder if she would ever see him again.

# Chapter 27

Marjorie woke in the middle of the night. Something in her dream had disturbed her, and now she couldn't remember what it was.

*Oh dear, it's so frustrating.*

She got up and made herself a cup of camomile tea. Perhaps that would help clear her mind.

Marjorie recalled the events of the previous night. The night had been beautiful, and she had been remembering many of the happy strolls that she and Ralph had taken in the past. One particular night had come to her mind.

It had been their diamond wedding anniversary a week before their final cruise together, and they had kept it low profile, having just a few close friends round for dinner. Ralph had said he would take her out for a special dinner on their cruise and, true to his word, that night he had wined and dined her as if they were in their twenties. He had been working hard and business worries had been concerning him, but on that night, he seemed to have left all of those concerns behind him.

After dinner, they had walked out on deck and he produced a small box from his pocket as they stood admiring the stars.

"I love you." It was a simple statement but Marjorie could see tears in his eyes as he looked at her. "I'm sorry if I've been a bit distracted. There's something going on in the business. I can't say much about it, but it's been a bit of a worry. Money is going missing and I think I know who is taking it." He had looked so sad. Marjorie just wanted to hold him. "Anyway, let's forget about that for now. Open your present."

She had opened the Tiffany box to see the most beautiful black diamond encrusted eternity ring. The stunning cut of the five diamonds almost took her breath away. Neither Ralph nor Marjorie was prone to extravagance, in spite of their wealth, which made the gift all the more special. She had taken the 24 carat gold ring out of the box and looked on the inner side at Ralph's request to find the engraving: RS, MS, 60 years.

She looked at the ring now and remembered that wonderful evening. Two months after that, Ralph was dead.

Marjorie brought her thoughts back to the previous night again. After recalling that wonderful night and admiring the precious ring on her left ring finger, she had felt a sudden shiver. She wasn't sure whether it was the sadness of her loss or remembering Ralph's business concerns that had caused it, but she had decided to return to her room.

In her dream she had seen herself walking purposefully along the deck towards the steps. It was at that moment she had sensed she wasn't alone and turned to look behind her. She felt herself falling again, and then she saw Rachel reaching out for her. But now she remembered what had woken her. As she had turned her head, she had felt the push, and at the same time she saw the inside of a man's left wrist underneath a black jacket.

*How odd*, she had thought as she fell, *no watch*.

Now, as she remembered that small detail, she wondered whether it was important.

*Perhaps it was, perhaps it wasn't.*

Her mind now turned to what Ralph had said about money going missing from the company. He had never mentioned it again, and she had learned over their sixty years of happy marriage not to pry. He would tell her when he was ready, but that opportunity had not arisen. His health had deteriorated rapidly on his return to work, resulting in the fatal heart attack.

*Who was taking money from the company? Is that what my Solicitor wants to talk to me about on my return? If it is Jeremy, it doesn't make sense that he keeps asking for more money to inject into the business. Is he just spending it on his extravagant lifestyle and his even more extravagant wife?*

Marjorie got back into bed and decided to take one of the sleeping tablets Dr Bentley had prescribed. She was determined to take much more of an interest in the firm when she got back to London. She would find out who was taking money and then sell up if that's what was required; she didn't need the money. The one thing she wasn't going to allow was her husband's work to be wasted on spongers and thieves.

# Chapter 28

*This blasted job's becoming impossible! How could that woman keep surviving? If I believed in fate, I would think that it's just not meant to be. No. Don't be stupid, it has just been bad luck, and now it's going to be nigh on impossible to get near to the old girl.*

Once again, he contemplated leaving the job undone and taking the risk on how it might affect his reputation. There was more to it than that though. There was his pride. He had *never* failed, and he couldn't accept failure of any kind now. His dad had been a complete failure – a weakling who allowed people to tread all over him. He had despised the way his dad was always polite to people, even when they scorned him, and was determined never to let people use him in the same way. Killing for a living empowered him. He was always in control, having the ability to take away life whenever he chose, and that's what motivated him above all else.

If he let this woman live, he could pretend it had been his own choice to his friends (not that he had that many), but deep down, he would always know that it had been his only failure. He would not be able to live with that, and even more importantly, it made him afraid of how it might affect him when it came to future jobs.

He had to finish the job, in spite of the risks. It just had to be done.

He had ignored the numerous calls he'd received yesterday in Gibraltar.

*He will just have to wait. I will tell him when it's done. Now I have that young woman to contend with as well.*

The tension was building in his temples. A job that had seemed like easy money was becoming the worst job of his life. It was bad enough that all his other hits seemed to be deserving of death whereas this one was not on that level and challenged what was left of his conscience. Now he would have to tread very carefully so that he wasn't recognised while finishing this elusive woman off.

*She's a strong old bird, I'll give her that. She should have died of fright by now.*

He had watched the stewards move the old lady's luggage from her room and seen where they had taken it, noticing the guard outside her new room.

*Well, he looks dopey enough, I can deal with him and then push her overboard.*

It was the only way he could see of getting the job done. He knew it would be risky, but he was starting to feel desperate. Anxiety was never a good sign for a hitman. The sooner he got this job done, the better.

*Tonight*, he thought as he tucked into a fried breakfast in the buffet.

# Chapter 29

Rachel availed herself of the opportunity to eat breakfast on the balcony of her new suite. The balcony was at least three times the size of the one in the previous stateroom and faced the sea behind the ship. She could see the foam the *Coral Queen* left behind and the waves eventually re-forming after being broken by the onward journey. The weather was still hot as the ship had entered the Atlantic and was off the west coast of Spain and Portugal. They would begin crossing the Bay of Biscay this evening and would be in Southampton in two days, docking at five in the morning.

Rachel's butler had been attentive, obviously under strict instructions to make sure that she had everything she required. He had introduced himself as Jeeves and for a moment she'd thought he was being serious, but then he explained his name was Mario. He looked and sounded Spanish, but explained that he was actually from El Salvador.

"I have wife in San Salvador and send money each month for family food," he explained in broken English.

"You must miss them," said Rachel, who had then been shown a number of photographs of his wife and three little boys, all under six. *It's perhaps as well you work away*, Rachel thought, but not unkindly. "Is Lady Snellthorpe awake?"

"Yes, ma'am. I have just taken her tea, she asked how you are."

"Will you tell her I will visit soon?"

Rachel turned away, not wanting to appear rude, but she needed some time to herself. Mario cleared the breakfast tray and left her in peace.

She was pleased to have free Wi-Fi and had been able to email her boss the previous evening to let him know that she would not be on street patrol on Monday, explaining why. Now she logged into her email account and found a reply.

*"Dear PC Prince,*

*That's the last time you are allowed to go away on holiday! I have made arrangements for you to work alongside the desk sergeant for next week and PC Gabriel will cover your shifts. I have attached your new rota.*

*See you Monday at eight o'clock sharp.*

*Regards*

*Sergeant Smythe."*

*Short and to the point, as ever,* she thought as she read through the email. *At least he attempted a joke.*

Rachel was not keen on desk duty; she enjoyed being out on the beat, but being a policewoman involved everything from emergency call outs to routine to the downright boring. She was pleased to have the email to her boss out of the way, and now she only had to work out how she was going to get to and from work for the next six weeks until the plaster could come off.

Her mind came back into the present and she logged off the computer and hobbled to Marjorie's room. Ravanos was sitting in the corridor and stood to attention when she passed. She smiled at him as she knocked on Marjorie's door.

Marjorie welcomed her in with a brisk hug and a kiss on the cheek.

"Hello, my dear. How are you feeling?"

"A lot better for a good night's sleep," Rachel replied.

"Would you like a cup of tea? Mario has just brought in a fresh pot."

"Yes please."

Rachel followed her out onto the balcony and joined her at the table.

"How do you like your room?" The old lady asked. Rachel smiled. "Sheer luxury, I wish I could enjoy it for longer."

"I remembered something in the night – well two things, actually. One is about the other night and one is more personal."

"Oh?" said Rachel, and she waited for Marjorie to continue.

"The first is that I remembered seeing the man who pushed me's left wrist. It seemed odd that he wasn't wearing a watch with a dinner suit. At least, I think it was a dinner suit. I noticed a black jacket cuff."

Rachel pondered this information for a moment. "Well, it could be he doesn't wear a watch, or it could be he was left-handed."

"Exactly what I thought! I think he was reaching out to push me with his left hand, but when I turned, he used his other hand. It all happened in a split second, but at least it might help narrow the field a little."

Marjorie seemed to be enjoying playing detective, and it was nice to see her more like herself again.

"All we need to do now is find a left-handed man with murder on his mind." Rachel poured herself another cup of tea. "What about the other thing?" she asked gently.

"Not long before my husband died, he had mentioned he thought someone was taking money from the business and that he knew who it was. I haven't thought about it since because I was too busy trying to cope with his death and then I had a lot of other matters to attend to. I left the business side of things to my son, Jeremy." Marjorie paused before continuing. "It might be Jeremy who has been taking money out of the business. Ralph was furious that he was too extravagant, spending well beyond his means. I think, after my husband died,

Jeremy thought he would be in full control of the company, but Ralph named me as controlling partner."

"How did he react to that?"

"How Jeremy reacts to most things, like a bull in a china shop. It took a while for him to accept it, but I thought he had come round. Now I have this awful feeling in the pit of my stomach that my son wants me dead, but I hardly dare imagine it." Marjorie's face set with a new determination. "But this old lady is not that easy to get rid of and I will fight any abuse of my husband's fortune until my dying breath."

Rachel reached for Marjorie's hand, unable to find words to respond. Everything in her wanted to protect this dear woman from whatever and whoever wanted to harm her. A deep anger that she had never felt before made her determined to get to the bottom of this before anything else happened. Unlike CSO Waverley, Rachel was certain the killer would try again. He had already killed an unsuspecting old lady, and she had no doubt that wasn't the end of it. Hitmen had to see their work through or they would not be hired again. Rachel knew how it worked.

"I will get a message to CSO Waverley about the possibility of our man being left-handed. Do you want me to mention your son?"

"No, dear. I think that is something I will need to investigate with Randolph, our Lawyer, when I return home."

After her tea with Marjorie, Rachel told Ravanos what Marjorie had told her and asked him to pass this information on to the CSO. She then decided to enjoy one of the many films that were available for free on her suite's TV, but halfway through *The Greatest Showman* she drifted off to sleep.

A distant ringing sound broke into her sleep and it took her a while to realise that it was the telephone in her room.

"Hello," she mumbled, fighting sleep.

"Rachel! Are you alright?" Sarah sounded stressed. "I just wanted to check in with you before I go back to work. It's been bedlam today with accidents and people running out of medication."

"Don't worry about me, I'm fine. I think I will ask Mario to find me some lunch and then sleep some more before trying to hunt down Carlos at dinner tonight. Hey, I didn't ask about your date the other night?"

"It was good, and I think there will be more dates on the next sailing as we are both with this ship for the foreseeable future. I wanted to let you know that Waverley has drawn a blank on suspects and your knight in shining armour still hasn't come forward."

"No-one with a criminal record?"

"Yes, there are several, but none of them fit the profile of a professional killer willing to do away with old ladies. We have a jewellery thief, a fraudster, a wife beater and a juvenile drug user. There are fifty-three that haven't come through yet. As you can imagine, trying to find the criminal records of three and a half thousand passengers and eighteen hundred crew is not easy."

"I didn't realise he would be looking at crew members."

"He's prioritised those who joined the ship in Southampton, but I think it is unlikely to be a crew member."

"I agree," said Rachel. "Marjorie saw a jacket cuff which suggests a passenger to me. Anyway, she is going to stay in her room tonight so she should be safe."

"That's good. I'll call you after I finish shift tonight. I hope it goes well with Carlos."

"Thanks, speak later."

Rachel hung up, smiling at the thought of seeing Carlos at dinner.

# Chapter 30

Rachel dressed up as well as she could for a woman wearing a plaster cast on her leg. She smiled at how she looked in the mirror. The dress she had chosen was sky blue cotton with long chiffon sleeves that would help to hide her arm dressing and the underlying wounds. From the knees up, she looked like a glamorous young woman enjoying a cruise holiday, but the plaster cast on her left lower leg reminded her that this was no ordinary cruise.

She applied the finishing touches to her makeup and added a lip gloss rather than lipstick, which complemented her full red lips. Once satisfied, she called Marjorie to let her know that she might be late back tonight and agreed to see her for coffee in the morning. Feeling a flutter of excitement at the thought of seeing Carlos again, she picked up her handbag and left the room.

Ravanos was seated in the corridor and he smiled at her. "Enjoy your evening, ma'am."

"Thank you, I will." She thought how boring it must be for him being on guard duty the whole time, but she hoped that his watch would remain boring as any activity would mean another attempt on Marjorie's life. She shuddered at the thought, and for a brief moment, wondered whether she should stay behind.

*Don't be silly that's his job.*

There was a queue for the lifts as people were making their way down for dinner, but Rachel managed to squeeze into one after a group of three people almost carried her along in their haste to make sure they got in. The lifts at this time of the evening were claustrophobic as people insisted on filling every square inch, not wanting to wait the extra few minutes for the next one to arrive. The majority were heading for the deck four restaurant, as was Rachel, but she decided to exit on deck six so that she could make her way through midships and then down the stairs.

This was the first time she had walked slowly along deck six, passing through the casino. As soon as she entered, she saw a familiar figure at the blackjack table. He looked different because he was sporting a moustache so she thought she was mistaken initially, but as he lifted his head, she recognised the eyes immediately.

He seemed unsure whether to acknowledge her at all. *Perhaps he doesn't recognise me,* she thought. She walked towards him and he smiled.

"Good evening."

"Good evening. I'm sorry to interrupt, but are you the gentleman who helped me and my friend the other evening?"

"Your friend?" He seemed momentarily startled. "Yes, of course, now I remember. You had both fallen." Other players were starting to listen in on their conversation as he spoke. "Oh dear, I seem to have lost again. Perhaps you would like to join me for a drink?" He picked up his chips and put them into his pocket before taking her by the arm.

"I was just heading for dinner, but yes, perhaps a quick drink."

They walked in uncomfortable silence towards a quiet wine bar where he ordered himself a cognac and Rachel a martini and lemonade. He then steered her towards a quiet corner.

"Did you not hear the announcements requesting you go to reception with regard to the accident?" Rachel took a sip of the drink he had bought her.

"I have to admit, I did hear the announcements, but I have been busy enjoying ship life. I hardly ever get away, you see." He smiled, but the smile didn't reach his eyes. "I wouldn't be able to help anyway, I didn't see anything."

"I see. Well, I must go, I'm meeting someone for dinner."

"Please finish your drink, and I promise I will go to reception with you afterwards if it helps."

As Rachel took another few gulps of her drink, she noticed that he picked his drink up with his left hand, and there was no watch on his left wrist. Her heart beating faster within her chest, she rose to leave, but began to feel confused and woozy, not knowing where she was. Feeling herself becoming more and more drowsy, she tried to stand, but her legs wouldn't carry her.

When she approached him in the casino, he tried to ignore her, but when she said that the old lady was her friend, he improvised. This whole business had been one shambolic mess after another. Now as he looked at her legs giving way under her, he was in turmoil over what to do next. He could just leave her there and go and finish off the old lady, but that wouldn't work now. The croupier knew who he was and had seen him with this young woman. Questions would be asked and they would find him. No, he would have to kill her as well.

*Collateral damage.* He sighed. *Such a shame, she is so beautiful.*

He had to remain professional, but he could feel beads of sweat appearing on his forehead. This young woman hadn't been part of the plan.

He waited for most of the people to leave the bar as they headed off to their various dinner activities. Seizing his moment while the bartenders were clearing away a large number of wine bottles and glasses from tables at the far end of the bar, he lifted Rachel from her seat, putting his left arm around her waist and picking up her handbag with his right hand. He half carried her along the corridor, speaking to her as if she was drunk while doing his best not to draw any attention to himself. It wasn't too difficult; most people were wrapped up in their own little worlds, so the few people who were still around barely cast a second glance.

"Almost there, darling." He spoke to her as an elderly couple gave him a sympathetic glance. Managing to get her to the lifts at the bow of the ship, he decided to take her up to deck fourteen. They could walk along the deck and take the rear lift up to fifteen.

*It is going well so far*, he thought as he began to calm down. He took out a pair of false spectacles from his pocket and added a beard, using the mirror in the lift. He didn't want anyone to recognise him.

The woman let out a moan and tried to pull away, but she wasn't strong enough.

"I'm sorry you had to be involved in this, but it will soon be over," he said.

They arrived at deck fourteen and he took the port side first. The stewards were busy restocking rooms and turning down beds so he felt secure they hadn't been noticed. Once they got to midships, he moved over to the starboard side to walk the rest of the way to the rear. They met one young couple on the way, but they were too busy kissing and giggling to notice him. The girl gave Rachel a quick glance, but then looked away.

By the time they reached the rear lifts, he was feeling a little bit out of breath. He decided to rest for a moment and sat the young woman down on the floor while he composed himself for the next part of the plan. All he had to do now was deal with the security officer on the next floor and hope the butler wasn't around.

Having gathered himself together, he lifted the drugged woman from the floor and entered the lift. He could feel adrenaline pumping through his body as he moved in for the kill. The woman was murmuring again and starting to struggle a bit more. She hadn't drunk the full dose, but the effects of the drug should last for a bit longer.

"Not long now," he said as he pulled her tightly towards him.

The lift doors opened, and he carried her out. He decided to pick her up and approach the end of the corridor where the security guard was seated.

The guard look surprised.

"Drunk too much. Hold onto her for a minute, will you?"

With that, he handed her over to the surprised guard, who almost dropped her. As he bent to catch her, the man picked up the chair and hit him over the head with it.

He left the woman on the floor, opening her door with her key card and dragging the unconscious security officer inside. Tying him up, he left the guard there. He was happy with his disguise; the guard would not have seen him for long enough to provide a detailed description, and even if he did, the first thing he would have noticed was the beard.

Moving quickly to pick up the chair and put it back in place, he lifted Rachel up off the floor and headed towards the old woman's room. He knocked on the door and held Rachel up in front of the spy hole.

It worked. The old woman opened the door.

"One word and she's dead," he said.

Rachel could hear noises piercing her brain. She could feel herself being carried along, but couldn't make any sense of what was happening. There was pain in her foot and her head was throbbing. She was trying to count the number of throbs: one, two, three, four, ouch! The pain in her head again.

Blurred corridors passed through her subconscious, but everything seemed unreal, like a piece of abstract art. She could feel an arm around her waist and tried to call Carlos, but sensed it wasn't Carlos holding her.

She felt the pain in her ankle again and could just about work out that she was on the floor. A shadow was dragging another shadow away, and now she was being held up outside a door. Her vision was returning, but things still appeared blurred.

*Marjorie?*

She felt herself being thrown onto a bed and she could hear voices.

"What have you done to her?" Marjorie's voice sounded distant, but Rachel could make out the words.

"Just a little drug. It's best for her in the long run."

"You're the man from the car, aren't you? So you're the one who has been trying to kill me." Marjorie sounded calm.

"Yes, and it hasn't been easy."

"Who is paying you? I will pay you double to cancel the job."

"Sorry, lady. That's not how it works. A contract is a contract and I have a reputation to live up to."

"I would still like to know who is paying you."

"I won't say."

"What now?"

"You both go overboard."

Rachel's brain started to come back to reality. She opened her eyes and saw him reaching out to grab Marjorie. Reaching for the fruit bowl, she picked it up and threw it with all her might.

"Damn!" the man shouted, blood on his face. "Looks like she will have to go first."

Rachel saw him push Marjorie out towards the balcony, then he turned on her. She felt him dragging her along the floor. The noise of the sea sounded much louder in her head and the pain in her ankle was excruciating.

Marjorie had been pushed to the floor and was struggling to get up. Rachel felt herself being lifted up and carried towards the barrier. She fought, but her strength wasn't there. Her mind was still numb and her limbs were struggling to co-ordinate.

*It's now or never*, she thought as the man heaved her up.

# Chapter 31

Sarah was finishing up her paperwork when Brigitte popped her head around the door.

"There's a Carlos Jacobi here to see you, Sarah."

She went into the waiting room and saw the handsome Carlos standing there.

"Hello. I'm Sarah."

"I'm sorry to bother you, but I was hoping to see Rachel this evening. I waited at dinner, but she didn't arrive. I thought you might know where she is."

"She said she was going to dinner as usual and she was hoping to see you, too."

Sarah was worried. She picked up the telephone and called Rachel's room, but there was no reply. She then tried Lady Snellthorpe.

"Hello."

"Hello, Lady Snellthorpe, it's Sarah. Have you seen Rachel?"

"No dear, she called me at six o'clock and said she would probably be late tonight. I think she was going to see that young man. Is everything alright?"

"Yes, all's good, I just wanted to catch her, that's all. Is everything quiet with you."

"Yes, everything's fine. There's someone at the door, so I'd better go, dear. It's probably the guard telling me he's changing shifts."

The phone went dead. Sarah looked at Carlos and shook her head.

"She was going to meet you. Come on, let's go and see if we can find her. Lady Snellthorpe is okay."

They went back to the restaurant, but people were now going in for the second sitting. Sarah asked the Maître D' to keep a lookout for Rachel and page her if she came in. Carlos looked worried sick, but he was holding it together for now.

"Let's just try the bars in case she's fallen asleep. The painkillers have been making her a bit tired. If no-one has seen her, I will contact security. They may want to put out a ship-wide alert."

They had been through every bar on deck's four and five when finally they entered the wine bar and gave a description of Rachel. The staff shook their heads until a Romanian bartender said he remembered a woman of that description coming into the bar with a man.

"They sat over there." He nodded his head in the direction of where Rachel had sat. "I thought it was odd because she only had one drink, but he was almost carrying her out. I only noticed them leave because I dropped a glass and saw out of the side of my eye. Is that how you say it?"

"Which way did they go?" Sarah was not inclined to give an English lesson at this moment.

"Towards elevators, bow."

"Thank you," said Sarah, and then she relented. "And it's out of the *corner* of my eye." The bartender smiled.

"Where would they go?" asked Carlos.

"I don't know. Come on, we'll go to her suite. I carry a ship-wide door pass." She turned back to the bartender. "Would you call security and tell them Rachel Prince has been abducted and we are heading to her room? Do you understand?"

The bartender picked up the phone as they left. Sarah could feel the adrenaline pumping through her body, and she could see that Carlos was also tense. They took the lifts to the fifteenth deck and Sarah opened Rachel's suite door. They immediately saw the security officer, Ravanos, tied up on the floor. He was just regaining consciousness, but they left him for now and ran towards Lady Snellthorpe's room.

Sarah unlocked the door and followed as Carlos rushed in. Rachel was being lifted up onto the balcony. Carlos ran towards her as the man turned, but Sarah could see that he wouldn't make it in time.

Just then, she saw Rachel's leg do a somersault, and the man went overboard. Carlos rushed over to Rachel and picked her up. Carrying her into the room, he laid her gently on the bed. Sarah was relieved to find Lady Snellthorpe sitting on the floor of the balcony, looking shaken but unharmed.

"Well, I have to say, I am pleased to see you." The old lady smiled at Sarah as the younger woman helped her to her feet.

"Are you hurt?" Sarah asked.

"No, dear, just shaken. He was going to kill us both, you know."

Sarah nodded and put her arm around Lady Snellthorpe, helping her through to the suite as six security guards came rushing into the room, CSO Waverley at the front. Rachel was sitting up on the bed.

"Man overboard," said Sarah quietly. The CSO got on his radio while the other officers checked the balcony. "And one of your officers is tied up in Rachel's room."

# Chapter 32

As Rachel saw Carlos running towards her, she knew he wouldn't make it in time. Hanging over the edge of the balcony with the man leaning over her, she drew her plastered leg back and gave one almighty kick which thrust upwards, catching his leg. The man lost his balance and dropped her before tumbling over the edge and down into the dark, black sea.

Momentarily, Rachel saw Sarah picking Marjorie up after she was whisked into the arms of Carlos. He carried her over to the bed and laid her down gently.

Rachel explained what had happened, how she had recognised the man in the casino and how he had lured her for a drink. She said how she had noticed he was left-handed just before the drug took effect, and that she couldn't remember anything else until she reached Marjorie's suite.

The man-overboard siren had sounded, and the ship had stopped, but Sarah explained it would be unlikely the man would be found as they hadn't called it straight away. The majority of the security officers were using searchlights to see if they could spot any sign of the man, but it was a futile search and impossible to find him in the dark. Rachel almost felt sorry for him until she remembered that he had intended to kill both her and Marjorie.

Sarah had made coffee for everyone although she handed Marjorie a glass of brandy as well.

"Does this mean we won't find out who was behind this?" asked Marjorie, sipping her brandy.

"Not necessarily," said Carlos, producing a phone from his pocket. "He dropped this when he fell and I caught it automatically when I reached for Rachel. I think it's a burner phone, and if we can unlock it, I suspect it will lead us to another burner phone."

Marjorie and Sarah looked confused. "Criminals use burner phones for illegal activities," Rachel explained. "They are untraceable and discarded after a job is done."

Waverley took the phone. "I will get onto it at once." He started to leave the room with a bounce in his step before turning back. "Does anyone know who that man was?"

"No, sorry," said Rachel. "He was playing blackjack, though, so someone from the casino might know his name. He also paid for the drinks in the bar with his room card, a cognac and a martini and lemonade."

Waverley smiled. "I think I will be offering you a job soon, young lady."

As he left the room, Rachel looked around at the three people who were now as close to her as anyone could be.

"You were marvellously calm," she said to Marjorie. "Even through my disorientated and muddled state, I could hear the calmness in your voice. How did you do it?"

"Ralph always said it wasn't British to be over emotional, and I thought if this was going to be my last few minutes on earth, I wanted my husband to be proud of me."

"He would be very proud. I think your attitude unnerved the man, and it brought me to my senses out of the fogginess of the drug."

"I am so pleased that you are safe, though, Rachel. I wouldn't have been able to live with myself if he had managed to—" Marjorie took another drink. "Although I wouldn't have lived anyway, would I?"

They all laughed, and it relieved some of the tension in the room.

Rachel smiled at Sarah and Carlos. "How did you know to come here?"

"It's a long story," said Sarah. "We have Carlos to thank for that."

"And a Romanian bartender," said Carlos.

The captain's voice came over the loudspeaker. "We are starting up the engines again, ladies and gentleman.

Do enjoy the rest of your evening on board the *Coral Queen*."

The room went silent as they realised what this meant. Rachel reflected soberly that she had killed a man, and it wasn't a pleasant thought.

"That nurse did warn me the plaster was hard and not to kick anybody," she said ruefully.

Both Sarah and Carlos squeezed her hands in acknowledgement.

"You couldn't have saved him." Carlos poured her a drink of brandy. "It was you or him."

# Chapter 33

Carlos helped Rachel back to her room. Her ankle was throbbing after being dragged along corridors and from kicking her assailant. Sarah stayed with Marjorie while the butler cleared her suite and then joined Rachel.

"Is she okay?" asked Rachel.

"Yes. She has had three brandies so I think she will sleep very well. She will either feel better or worse once we know who is behind all this."

Sarah and Carlos left Rachel to get some sleep. In spite of all the excitement, she drifted off into a deep sleep, only slightly aware of the pain in her ankle after taking some pain killers. Sarah had told her Dr Bentley would probably want to do another X-ray in the morning to make sure it hadn't been damaged.

The next morning, Marjorie joined Rachel for breakfast, and Sarah arrived shortly afterwards with Carlos and CSO Waverley.

"We have cracked the phone code, and the captain is heading towards shore so that we can get a satellite signal to call the number. There is only one number on the phone and that will be the one."

"What's the plan?" asked Rachel.

"We are going to text the number to say that the job is done. We have read previous texts and have picked up the general tone of the way the man speaks. His name was Stefano Davidson, and he is officially missing, presumed dead. We have gone through his room, but there is not a lot to go on, except that we now have his bank details. He texted them to the person employing him. He probably has numerous accounts, but I'm sure this will be the one he is paid into."

Waverley paused for a moment.

"Is there something wrong?" asked Rachel.

He looked at Marjorie, who responded, "Out with it, man!"

"Because we don't know who is responsible, after we have sent the text," he coughed, "Dr Bentley will need to call your son and tell him you have met with a tragic accident. This will not be pleasant for him, unless—"

"Unless he is responsible." Looking pale, Marjorie finished the sentence for him.

"Yes, ma'am."

"I don't think we have any alternative, do we?"

Rachel took Marjorie's hand. "Coffee?" she asked.

"Make it strong," the old lady replied.

Beeping from all their phones broke the silence as a satellite signal brought them to life. "Okay, let's do this," said Waverley, tapping into the phone: "*Job done, transfer money.*"

Two minutes later, a reply came through.

"*About time! Once confirmed will transfer payment. Remember to destroy phone.*"

Waverley typed again. "*Will destroy once money transfer confirmed. You do the same.*"

"*Do they think it's an accident?*"

"*Yes, no investigation.*"

"*Will let you know when money transferred.*"

"Right, now it's Dr Bentley's turn," said Waverley. As he left the room, he turned and added, "I will let you know when there are any developments. The captain will stay within satellite range for as long as he can."

Sarah went back to work after Rachel agreed she would have an X-ray once things settled down, and Rachel, Marjorie and Carlos decided to play gin rummy. Marjorie had offered to return to her room, but as much as Rachel would have liked to have been alone with Carlos, she was not going to let Marjorie sit alone, waiting for news.

Carlos was the perfect gentleman, and he brightened them both up, reminding Marjorie of some of the jobs he had done for her husband in the past. She seemed to enjoy the reminiscences.

"I am so sorry that I didn't look after you properly on this trip. I was told it was a babysitting role really, and that you were unlikely to be in any real danger. I let my guard down when I saw the ship's security watching out for you."

"I have to ask," said Marjorie, "who did hire you?"

"I shouldn't really say, but I suppose there's no harm you knowing now. It was your Lawyer, Randolph, but he hired me on behalf of someone else."

"And who might that someone be?"

Carlos' phone rang. "It's Randolph, I guess the news is out. I think I'd better answer it to keep up the charade for now." He pressed answer. "Hello."

Carlos left the room for around fifteen minutes. When he returned, Rachel waited patiently for him to explain.

"The news is out. I'm in the doghouse for allowing you to be killed, Lady Snellthorpe. Randolph says that Jeremy took it badly. I felt guilty lying to him, to be honest, but we need everyone to think the killer was successful so that whoever is responsible can feel relaxed."

Rachel looked at Marjorie who was visibly shaking now.

"I don't think it was your son," said Carlos, taking her hand.

"Why not?" asked Rachel, horrified that he might be raising false hopes in this tender lady's heart.

"Because Randolph just told me, I would have to answer to Jeremy when I got back. That it was he who paid Randolph to hire me."

The relief on Marjorie's face was obvious, and she allowed the tears that she had been holding back to fall. Rachel hugged her.

At that moment the door opened and in came the captain, Waverley, Dr Bentley and Sarah. They were looking pleased.

"The plan worked," said Waverley. "The money was transferred half an hour ago, and we have traced it back to a Phillip Mason."

Marjorie gasped. "He is financial director of the company."

"And he is being arrested as we speak. I think that investigators will find that he has been siphoning money from the company for a while, and he was obviously getting desperate for more."

"He was Ralph's oldest friend and would become joint controlling partner in the event of my death to prevent my son overspending," Marjorie explained. "No wonder Ralph looked sad. I thought he suspected Jeremy, but this would have been worse for him. Randolph told me that Ralph had planned to change his will, but died before he could do it."

"That explains it, then," said the captain. "I am so sorry, Lady Snellthorpe, for all you have gone through, and to you, Miss Prince. The cruise line will try to make it up to you in some small way, I assure you."

"Thank you, Captain." Marjorie was ever the lady.

"I have just got off the phone to your son again, Lady Snellthorpe," said Dr Bentley. "Despite giving me a piece of his mind, he is relieved that you are alive and well. He apologises for having been so distant and cold recently, but he has been so worried about the company seemingly leaking money and hadn't wanted to worry you. He said to tell you he is looking forward to dinner on Tuesday?"

Marjorie smiled. "That is our weekly dinner date. I expect this one could be interesting."

After all the events of the day, Rachel was pleased to be left alone at last. She stood out on the balcony, peering into the night sky then she stared at the letter in her hand.

"Goodbye, Robert," she said as she let it drop unopened into the ocean.

With a sigh of relief, she returned to the stateroom and got into bed, reflecting on the day. Marjorie had given her an open invitation to stay with her at any time. The captain had told her the cruise line was offering her a free luxury-suite cruise to a destination of her choosing, and a cruise-line representative had offered her a healthy sum by way of compensation on condition she signed a gagging order. Marjorie had been offered free cruises for life and an undisclosed sum of money for the trauma she had suffered. In addition to this, CSO Waverley had offered Rachel a job as a security officer if she wanted to take him up on it.

*Best of all,* Rachel thought as she put her head to her pillow for the last time on board the *Coral Queen*, *Carlos has asked me out on a date.*

## THE END

# Thank you

If you have enjoyed reading this book, **please leave an honest review on Amazon and/or any other platform that you may use.** I read all reviews and love it when someone likes my work – it makes my day!

## Connect with me

www.dawnbrookespublishing.com

www.facebook.com/dawnbrookespublishing

www.twitter.com/dawnbrookes1

www.pinterest.com/dawnbrookespublishing

# Other Books by Dawn Brookes

## Rachel Prince Mysteries

*A Cruise to Murder*
*Deadly Cruise*
*Killer Cruise*
*Dying to Cruise*
*A Christmas Cruise Murder*
*Murderous Cruise Habit*
*Honeymoon Cruise Murder*

## Memoirs

*Hurry up Nurse: memoirs of nurse training in the 1970s*
*Hurry up Nurse 2: London calling*
*Hurry up Nurse 3: More adventures in the life of a student nurse*

## Coming Soon

Book 8 in the Rachel Prince Mystery Series
*A Murder Mystery Cruise*
Book 1 in the Carlos Jacobi PI Series
*Body in the Woods*

## Books for Children

Ava & Oliver's Bonfire Night Adventure
Ava & Oliver's Christmas Nativity Adventure
Danny the Caterpillar
Gerry the One-Eared Cat

# Body in the Woods

*A peaceful village. A hidden secret. A gripping new crime novel for 2020.*

When private investigator Carlos Jacobi spends the Christmas break with his sister in the Peak District, his dog uncovers a body in the woods. Why would someone kill a seemingly harmless old man? After Carlos is hired to investigate, he discovers that the dead man's family and people in the village have secrets in abundance.

Carlos had hoped he would never meet the man put in charge of the investigation again after their time in Afghanistan and has to face issues that still haunt him. The bad blood between them threatens to cloud the investigation as neither man can bury the past. D.I. Masters is livid when the dead man's family hire Carlos to investigate the death and orders his sergeant to make sure the private investigator is kept out of the loop.

Carlos unravels lies and motives among the seemingly innocuous village population. When his dog, *Lady* makes another grisly discovery, the case becomes more complex. Carlos teams up with an old friend to get to the bottom of a frustrating case.

*Murder and lies in the Peak District.*

*Bestselling author, Dawn Brookes does it again. The book is packed with rich characters, a deep and engaging plot that keeps you turning the pages.*
*A psychological masterpiece from a gifted author.*

# About the Author

Dawn Brookes is fun-loving and light-hearted as shown in her writing.

She writes across genres, but has developed a passion for cosy mysteries. The Rachel Prince Mystery series combines her love of cruising with a love of writing. This popular series frequently hits the bestseller charts and has a strong following. The surname of the protagonist is in honour of her childhood dog, *Prince*, who used to put his head on her knee while she lost herself in books.

Dawn is author of bestselling Book *Hurry up Nurse: memoirs of nurse training in the 1970s* following her life as a student nurse in Leicester, England. *Hurry up Nurse 2: London calling* follows the author to London where she undertakes specialist cardio-thoracic training. The third in the trilogy, *Hurry up Nurse 3: more adventures in the life of a student nurse* outlines the final leg in her training and is based in the south of England. Dawn worked as a hospital nurse, midwife, district nurse and community matron during a career that spanned thirty-nine years.

Before turning her hand to writing for a living, she had multiple articles published in professional journals and co-edited a nurse prescribing textbook.

Dawn grew up in Leicester, later moved to London and Berkshire and now lives in Derby. She holds a Bachelors degree with Honours and a Masters degree in education.

Dawn has a passion for nature and loves animals, especially dogs. Animals will continue to feature in her children's books as she believes caring for animals and nature helps children to become kinder human beings.

# Acknowledgements

Thank you to my beta readers for advice and encouragement regarding the early drafts. You know who you are!

Thanks to editor, Alison Jack for sharpening the text, pointing out errors and helping to make the book a better read.

Thanks to Zoe Gooding of Zedolus for proofreading the final draft.

Thanks to my friends who cruise with me regularly, without whom I would not have had the inspiration for the Rachel Prince Mystery series.

.

Made in the USA
Monee, IL
02 March 2023